A FAMILY FOR ⊣E ALIEN WARRIOR

TREASURED BY THE ALIEN 4

HONEY PHILLIPS
BEX MCLYNN

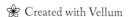 Created with Vellum

CHAPTER ONE

Mganak looked up from the filter he had been repairing when the proximity alarm sounded. While an artificial object in the vicinity meant the prospect of salvage, he was returning from a successful trip and in no immediate need of credits.

"What do you think, Sagat?" he asked the rajpar who had curled up in his usual nest of blankets to watch Mganak work. Sagat yawned widely, the overhead lights glinting on his fangs, then put his head back down.

"You're a big help," Mganak grunted, then sighed and went to check the scanners. *There.* An abandoned lifeboat floating close to a nearby asteroid. Since it wasn't emitting a signal, the occupants must be long gone—rescued or deceased. Either way, the ship itself should be worth a fair number of credits, and it was small enough that he could bring it into his cargo hold.

Switching to manual controls, he navigated closer until he could seize the vessel with the ship's grappling arm, then opened the outer doors to the hold. A few minutes and some careful maneuvering later, the small lifeboat was safely inside.

As he restored the oxygen levels in the hold, he briefly considered just leaving it there but curiosity got the better of him. He'd just give it a quick inspection before resuming his journey. If all it needed was a quick retrofit, he could begin the repairs on the way home.

From the outside, it appeared to be undamaged, and his hopes rose that it would only require a few simple repairs. There were no identifying markings, but that wasn't uncommon—the very fact that many ships used generic lifeboats was one reason why it should be an easy sale.

As he entered the small airlock, he was surprised to find the lifeboat still maintained a breathable atmosphere. But then again, they were designed to support life for an extended period of time. Hopefully, that meant the occupants had been rescued.

He slowly opened the inner door, already braced for what he might find. But instead of an empty vessel—or dead bodies— the ship was full of living beings. But it was the female directly in front of him who captured his attention. Shock held him motionless as he stared at her.

Since the plague that had devastated the Confederated Planets had disproportionately affected females, it was very rare to see one traveling in space, let alone one as attractive as this one. Big brown eyes stared up at him from a pale face covered with small golden specks.

She blazed with warmth and color in the dim interior of the vessel, from the quantity of bright red hair escaping from a futile attempt to confine it to a long gown of bright fabric that floated around her small curvy body. The cloud of fabric couldn't conceal the lush swell of her breasts—or the fact that she was pointing a blaster at him.

Despite the weapon, his body responded immediately to

her presence. He automatically stepped closer as her tantalizing scent reached him, his tail flicking in her direction.

A startled gasp made him drag his stunned gaze away from her long enough to check out the other inhabitants of the small vessel. A very young female gazed at him with wide eyes, her hands clasping the shoulders of an even younger male. A second, much older female regarded him with complete disdain. All of them appeared to be of the same race as the first female, but the final occupant was not. A very pregnant Vedeckian huddled against the wall, and he bit back a sigh.

"What the hell are all of you doing in here?"

WANDA'S HEART RACED AS SHE STARED UP AT THE GIANT green alien standing in the airlock of the lifeboat. The Vedeckians who had originally abducted her from Earth could almost pass for human at a distance. This male could never be mistaken for anything other than an alien. Textured green skin covered almost reptilian features with big, dark eyes and a thin mouth. Instead of hair, a series of ridges curved back over his head and down across his shoulders. His very broad shoulders. A tight-fitting dark shirt clung to an impressively muscled body, and the part of her that secretly devoured romance novels automatically responded.

Her gaze started to drift lower, to equally tight black pants, and she yanked it back up to his face, trying to decide what to do. She had been prepared to confront the Vedeckians, not this stranger. What was he going to do with them? Aside from his intimidating—and disturbingly exciting size—she didn't feel threatened, not even when he took a step closer.

"What the hell are all of you doing in here?"

The low, deep voice sounded more frustrated than angry, but her chin went up instinctively and she tightened her grip on the gun. At least the translator the Vedeckians had so painfully implanted in her head worked with this alien as well.

"We were abandoned," she said shortly.

"I do not understand. Was your ship in danger?"

"How should I know?" She scowled at him. "We were just prisoners. When the guards rounded us up and shoved us in here, they didn't bother to tell us why." And despite the cramped conditions and the eventual shortage of food, it had still been a hundred times better than being in a Vedeckian cell.

"Prisoners?" He sounded as if he'd never heard the word before.

"Yes, prisoners. Do you think we chose to be taken from our planet and shoved in a cell to be treated like animals?" Taking a deep breath, she lifted the weapon they had found in a concealed compartment in the lifeboat. "I demand to see the captain immediately."

Unfortunately, he looked almost amused now that his initial shock had faded. "You demand?"

She took a firmer grip on the gun. "Yes. We wish to be returned to our planet. Now I want to see the captain."

"You're looking at him. I am Captain Mganak Sar'Taren, and this is my ship, *The Wanderer*."

"My name is Wanda Peabody and I—*we* don't belong here. You will return us to our world," she said as confidently as possible.

He didn't seem to be listening. Instead, he looked from her face to the children and Alicia, and finally to Kareena. Her heart sank as he slowly shook his head.

"I cannot do that."

"What do you mean you can't do that?" She tightened her grip on the gun, praying that she wouldn't have to use it. "Aren't you forgetting that I'm the one who's armed?"

He shook his head again, then with an unbelievable flash of

4

speed, he snatched the gun out of her hand before she had time to react. Kareena gave a muffled scream, and she could swear she heard Alicia make a disgusted snort, but her eyes were focused on the stranger's face as she stepped protectively in front of the others. He still didn't look angry, but she knew how the Vedeckians had reacted to any sign of rebellion.

"Please. I'm the one who had the gun. They haven't done anything wrong. If you need to punish somebody, punish me."

Davy suddenly twisted out of his sister's grip and darted in front of Wanda. Little hands on his hips, he scowled fiercely up at the alien. "Don't touch."

Even though his sister had warned her not to touch the little boy without warning, Wanda automatically reached out to pull Davy back in case the alien reacted in anger. As soon as she put her hands on Davy, he started to keen and rock back and forth. Darla rushed over and urgently tried to reassure him. Alicia demanded that he keep quiet. Kareena cried. Wanda found herself giving the alien a despairing look.

He rubbed a hand across his face, looking remarkably frustrated.

"Quiet," he ordered.

His voice wasn't loud but it carried an unmistakable note of authority. Everyone except Davy went silent. The boy continued to rock, repeating "no, no" over and over.

To her shock, Mganak kneeled down so that he was closer to the boy's level. "Do not be afraid." When his words didn't seem to penetrate, the male looked at Darla. "What does he need?"

"Something to distract him." The girl shrugged a little helplessly. "He doesn't have his toys."

"Hmm." Mganak frowned, then dug in a pocket of his pants and pulled out a small tool of some kind. Holding it up so that Davy could see it, he opened and closed the parts until he caught Davy's attention. Then he placed it on his open palm and held it out to Davy.

Davy had stopped rocking, and now he reached out and picked up the tool. He turned it over in his hands, pulling out the various extensions and pushing them back in again, over and over. Relieved that he seemed calmer, Wanda turned back to Mganak. Hopefully, his patience with the boy was a good sign.

"I'm sorry I held the gun on you. I didn't know if you were another slaver. You're not, are you?"

"A slaver?" He looked appalled. "Of course not. Who would..." His gaze flicked to Kareena. "Did the Vedeckians take you?"

"Yes. And if you're not a slaver, how about you give me my gun back?"

"I am not going to let you carry a weapon on my ship. If you accidentally fired it and it penetrated the hull, we could all die." Ignoring her sudden pallor, he continued, "You will not need it. You are under my protection now."

Part of her was actually tempted to believe him, but she couldn't risk the safety of the others.

"That's very nice of you, but unless you're going to return us to our planet, we would prefer to be on our way." Not that they knew where they were going.

He shook his head. "I am not going to send females and children back out into space in a lifeboat that does not even have a working emergency beacon."

Fudge. It was bad enough that they had been set adrift, but to know that no one was even looking for them was a worse blow. Apparently, they weren't as valuable to the Vedeckians as she had assumed.

"Then what are you going to do with us?" she asked.

He sighed and rubbed his face again. "I don't know."

"If you would simply return us to our planet, then you wouldn't have to worry about it," Alicia said coolly, as if the alien was no more than a convenient chauffeur.

To Wanda's surprise, he tilted his head to one side and actually looked as if he was considering it for a moment. "Where is your planet located?"

"How would I know? Surely you have some kind of..." Alicia waved a dismissive hand. "Star map, or something?"

"I do indeed. But it doesn't come labeled with any signs indicating which planet is the home of a group of unfortunate females."

A faint line appeared between Alicia's perfectly arched brows, and Wanda's ember of hope was extinguished.

"Is there anyone who might know?" she asked, trying not to sound as desperate as she felt.

A warm band encircled her wrist, and she looked down to find the alien's tail wrapped around it. For some reason, she found it comforting rather than alarming. She must be going crazy. He didn't even seem to realize that it had happened until she started to tug her arm away. He looked shocked as he muttered a quick apology, but even then his tail seemed reluctant to release her, skating over her hand with a gentle caress, the textured surface both soothing and tantalizing.

He sighed. "There is a Patrol station on Ayuul. I suppose I could take you that far."

"Patrol? You mean like the police?" The word apparently didn't translate, and she tried again. "They represent the law?"

"Yes, that is correct. Although I still cannot guarantee that they will be able to locate your home world, at least they would have more references than I do." He frowned, then stepped to one side and gestured at the exit. "Can we continue this discussion outside? This space is uncomfortably small."

He had a point. It had been cramped with the five of them.

With the alien's massive body added to the mix, it seemed to have shrunk even further. She darted a quick look at the others. Alicia nodded, Darla looked scared but shrugged, and even Kareena nodded. That confirmed her decision. If the Vedeckian, who was scared of her own shadow, was willing to leave the lifeboat, it was probably safe.

Alicia led the way with her usual regal air while the children scrambled after her.

"You're sure about this?" Wanda murmured to Kareena as the Vedeckian passed her.

"No, but the Cire are an honorable race. Unlike my own," the other female added bitterly.

"I don't suppose we have much choice anyway." With a sigh she followed the others out, hoping their situation hadn't gone from bad to worse.

CHAPTER TWO

As Wanda stepped out of the lifeboat, she was overly aware of Mganak's body at her back, but she didn't feel threatened. A shiver of excitement danced down her spine at the sure knowledge that he was watching her. She forced herself to concentrate on the rest of her companions. Davy was still playing with the tool that Mganak had given him but the others were huddled together nervously. Even Alicia looked uncharacteristically anxious but she stood in front of the children in a protective pose.

The lifeboat had been placed in the center of a two-story space. Mesh cages lined the walls on all sides and her heart skipped a beat until she recognized that they were obviously designed to hold cargo. A second level held more of the storage cages behind a catwalk that led around the perimeter of the hold. On the rear wall, she could see two doors behind a set of steps that rose up to the catwalk. The space was rather cluttered and not exactly clean, but it was a welcome change from the depressing sterility of the Vedeckian ship.

"Now what?" Alicia asked, reverting to her normal coolness.

"I assume you would prefer actual bunks?" Mganak asked.

The lifeboat had been equipped with airline type seats that only partially reclined.

Alicia raised a skeptical brow. "In exchange for what?"

Before he could answer, Wanda caught a flash of movement from the rear of the hold, and a dark figure came slinking towards them. "Oh my God. What is that?"

As it drew closer, Wanda could see that it was some type of animal. It moved with the muscular grace of a big cat but had the extended snout and facial structure closer to that of a canine. A crown of flexible spikes covered its head and extended down its back to end in a barbed tail. As it drew closer, she could see that it was covered with fine scales in shades of dark blue with an underlying metallic sheen.

"This is Sagat. He is a rajpar," Mganak said calmly, smiling at the animal.

"Is he dangerous?"

"Of course. But only to those who wish him harm."

Sagat yawned, exposing a disturbing number of pointed teeth, then prowled forward. He circled their small group as they all stood frozen until he came to Davy. After contemplating the child thoughtfully, he gave a low, throbbing purr. To her shock, Davy smiled and put his arms around the animal.

"I guess he likes children." Her smile felt shaky with relief.

"Apparently. He's never been around any before." Before she could ask any other questions, Mganak turned and led the way up the steps. She looked back at the others, but they were all watching her expectantly so with a slight shrug, she followed him.

Another door opened off the top landing into a short

corridor lined with doors. Mganak opened the first one to reveal a small cabin with bunk beds on one wall.

"Crew cabin."

"Bunk beds," Davy yelled as he raced into the room. "I get top."

He climbed the ladder and threw himself on the top bunk with a happy squeal. Sagat followed him, leaping easily from the floor up to the bunk before curling up next to the boy.

"I'm not sure that's a good idea," she said. Davy looked so small next to the big animal.

"Are you going to make it get down?" Darla asked sarcastically as she scowled and entered the cabin after her brother. "I guess we're staying in here."

"I'm not sure—"

"They will be fine," Mganak said gruffly as he opened the next door.

This cabin contained a single bed and a bank of white cabinets. Wanda shuddered. It was too similar to the Vedeckian ship for her liking.

"This was intended as a medical unit," Mganak said. "I never did get around to fully fitting it out. Still, it has a bed."

Alicia gave the blank white surroundings a disapproving look, but Kareena said softly, "I don't mind staying here. If no one else wants it."

"Are you sure?" Wanda asked.

"Yes, it's fine."

Wanda studied the other female's face, but she didn't look distressed. Perhaps she felt at home in the sterile environment.

"Guest cabin," Mganak announced as he opened the next door.

Another minimalist space awaited, but this one had a larger bed. Dark green carpet covered the floor and the walls were painted a paler shade. Alicia nodded. "This will do until we reach some type of civilization."

She walked in and shut the door firmly behind her.

Mganak frowned at the closed door.

"Is something wrong?" she asked.

"I had assumed that two of you would share that cabin."

"Does that mean you're out of rooms?" Her heart sank. As much as she hated to admit it, she had been looking forward to sleeping in an actual bed.

"No," he said shortly. "Follow me."

He led the way through a small but comfortable looking lounge. A counter separated what appeared to be a kitchen area from the rest of the room, which was cluttered with a table and some over-sized furniture. At the far end, another set of stairs led up to a second landing. One side of the landing opened to what was obviously the bridge of the ship, with two chairs facing an impressive bank of control panels. Both chairs were empty.

"Shouldn't someone be flying the ship?" she asked nervously.

He barked a laugh. "Autopilot. Although at the moment we are not in transit." Opening the door on the other side of the landing, he added, "You can stay here."

A short passage led past a small bathroom into a cabin dominated by a huge bed. But it wasn't the bed that caught her attention. Windows completely ringed the walls, showcasing a breathtaking view of space and the panorama of stars surrounding them.

"This is the first time I've really felt like I was in space," she murmured as she walked over to the windows. Perhaps the infinite display of stars surrounding her should have made her feel small and insignificant, but instead, she felt as if she was expanding outward to become part of this vast universe. A warm weight crept across her back, and she didn't have to look down to know that Mganak's tail was curled around her. But it didn't feel threatening. It felt like he was hugging her.

She didn't know how long they stood there in silence watching the stars before she finally shook her head and smiled up at him. "Thank you."

He wasn't watching the stars, he was studying her face, but then he too shook his head. His tail dropped away and left her feeling unexpectedly bereft as she forced another smile. "This is a wonderful—"

Her words broke off abruptly as she took another look around the cabin and realized that the bed was in disarray and there was a small collection of personal objects lining the shelves under the windows. "Is this your room?"

He shrugged, already heading for the door. "I will be down in the training room."

"But I don't want to take your room."

"Your room now." His words floated after him as he shut the door behind him, leaving her alone for the first time in weeks.

Her knees suddenly felt shaky, and she collapsed onto the bed. From what she could calculate, she had been in space for less than three weeks and she was on her third alien ship. How had any of this happened to her?

One minute she'd been walking home from her job in the library of her small town, enjoying the warm summer evening. The only thing on her mind had been trying to decide if she wanted to use an animal theme in the nursery she was decorating or to go with fairy tales instead. The sun had just set, and the scent of honeysuckle filled the air. The few streetlights in town were in the main business district but the gathering dusk didn't bother her. She'd walked this route almost every day for the past ten years, ever since she'd saved up enough of her modest salary to purchase the small bungalow.

Without warning, a sudden blaze of pain erupted in her shoulder. She'd had just enough time to wonder if she was having a heart attack before the world went black. The next thing she knew, she awoke on a narrow cot in a room with white metal walls.

Regarding her thoughtfully from a cot on the opposite wall was a slender, elegant older woman. Well-tailored white pants and a white linen shirt set off her rich brown complexion, and a chunky coral necklace perfectly matched her coral fingernail polish. Flecks of silver were sprinkled throughout her dark hair, neatly arranged in a short, stylish haircut. She looked so perfectly composed that Wanda automatically found herself trying to smooth back the red curls escaping from her braid and straighten out the rather rumpled dress she had chosen for story time with the preschool group.

The woman raised an eyebrow and Wanda blushed, then focused on more important matters. "What happened? Where are we?"

"As ridiculous as this may sound, I believe we have been captured by aliens," the woman said calmly in a low, well-modulated voice with a slight Southern drawl.

"You're kidding!"

"I'm afraid not." The woman gestured at the front of their... cell, and for the first time, Wanda realized that the front wall was made of clear glass. "You'll see them soon enough. They may even appear human at first, but I assure you they are not." She gave a delicate shudder.

"How long have you been here—I'm sorry, what's your name?"

"I am Alicia Palmer Kensington. And I believe I have been here for approximately twenty-four hours. There's no way to tell time, of course, but the lights dimmed for an extended period after I was brought on board."

The other woman could have been discussing the weather, and Wanda tried to mimic her calm. "I'm Wanda Peabody. It's nice to meet you."

"Indeed," Alicia said a little mockingly, and Wanda felt her cheeks heat again.

"Where are you from?"

"Savannah. And you?"

"Edgerton. South Carolina," she added when the other woman looked blank. "Not too far from Savannah, really. I'm a librarian."

Just saying the words made her heart ache. This couldn't be happening. Her life was exactly as she had planned. She loved her job, loved the small town where she lived and worked and where she knew so many of the inhabitants by name. She loved the cottage she had spent the past ten years restoring—everything from hand sanding the old heart pine floors to painting the intricate moldings with fresh white paint.

She had even found a solution for the only thing that was missing from her life: a child. The artificial insemination process had been successful, and she was four months pregnant. Now, in the blink of an eye, her perfectly ordered life had been completely upended. There had to be a way out of here, a way back to her life. Not just for her sake but more importantly, for her daughter's sake.

Alicia's eyes followed the movement when Wanda's hand automatically curved over her stomach.

"You're pregnant?"

"Yes."

For the first time the other woman's face softened. "I'm sorry," she said quietly. "Perhaps—"

A noise arose in the corridor, and Alicia stiffened. "Keep quiet and do not argue with them. They are not... kind."

A man appeared in the corridor. No, not a man, Wanda realized as she took a second look. His skin was as white and smooth as plastic, his hair matte black, but his eyes were the worst, glowing red and completely inhuman.

"Move away from the opening," he ordered. He wasn't speaking English, but she understood him all too clearly.

Up until this moment, a part of her had hoped that Alicia was wrong, that it was all some giant hoax, but he was all too real. Why? Why had they taken her? She wanted to demand answers, but Alicia's warning echoed in her head and she kept her mouth shut.

The glass wall at the front of the cell slid to one side and she heard a child's voice, not loud but frantically repeating "no, no, no" over and over. To hell with Alicia's warning. She instinctively headed for the distressed child. The alien shook his head and grabbed her arm with long, cold fingers. Six fingers, she realized just before he raised a device in his other hand and pressed it to her arm. The world exploded in a blaze of pain, and she collapsed to her knees, barely conscious.

A second alien shoved two children past her. A young girl, no more than ten or eleven, was carrying a younger child. He was rigid in her arms, his head thrashing back-and-forth as he repeated his litany.

As soon as they were inside the cell, the door closed again. The two aliens stood outside looking disdainfully at them. One of them shook his head. "I still don't see how this is going to make us any profit."

"You know the captain. He's always looking for opportunities. If this is successful, it means we don't have to specifically search out breeders or infants on each trip." The other male shrugged. "It would mean faster, easier trips."

"I can't see it myself. Who's going to pay for older children, let alone old females?"

"That's what Captain Kane wants to find out. He thinks there's a market for older children because they require less care. And older females..." He shrugged again. "You never know what will appeal to a buyer. I've always made a good profit when I've been part of his crew so I'm willing to give him the benefit of the doubt."

"I suppose. But I'd rather be looking at a cell full of young breeders."

"If this doesn't work out, you will be next time. This planet is ripe for the taking."

As the two males disappeared, the fiery pain finally started to subside and Wanda scrambled to her feet. The boy was still safe in the young girl's arms, and his cries had diminished. She had her arms wrapped tightly around him and she was rocking with him.

"Is he all right? Are you all right?" Wanda asked softly.

The girl glared at her suspiciously from behind long, stringy black hair. She was painfully thin, and Wanda suspected it was due to lack of food rather than just her youth. The boy in her arms also had dark hair, and she thought she detected a resemblance.

"Is he your brother? What's his name?"

The girl's arms tightened, but she eventually muttered, "Davy. And I'm Darla."

"Hi, Darla. I'm Wanda. And this is Alicia."

"Where are we?" Darla demanded. "Are those men wearing costumes?"

"I don't think so. I think they were aliens."

"You've gotta be fu—freaking kidding me."

"I know it sounds crazy, but I don't know if there's another explanation." She looked a little helplessly at Alicia.

"There isn't," Alicia said coolly. When Wanda glared at her, she shrugged. "I have always felt it best to confront reality. No matter how unpleasant."

"But why do they want us?" Darla asked desperately.

"I believe they intend to sell us."

Alicia again made no attempt to soften her statement, but Darla didn't flinch. She stuck her lip out pugnaciously. "Then they'd better sell us as a pair. I'm never leaving Davy."

Wanda suspected that the girl knew as well as they did that there would be nothing she could do to prevent the aliens from separating them.

"How come I can understand them?" Darla asked.

"It is some type of implant." Alicia winced and rubbed her neck, and Wanda realized that her neck ached as well. "I saw them inject you while you were unconscious. I was not so lucky."

"I don't remember." Darla stared down at her brother, who seemed to have fallen asleep. "But maybe that's what set Davy off. He doesn't like it when people touch him."

"I don't think they'll bother us in here," Wanda said optimistically.

Alicia raised an eyebrow but didn't contradict her, and they all relapsed into silence.

Wanda kept waiting for something to happen, for the aliens to reappear with more prisoners, but the corridor outside their cell remained empty. Eventually, the tension took its toll, and she drifted off into an exhausted sleep.

She awoke as one of the aliens reappeared and delivered four plastic boxes containing tasteless wafers. Remembering the baby, she forced herself to eat. Alicia picked at one but both children devoured them without complaint. Davy was stacking and unstacking the boxes when the alien came to collect them.

To Wanda's shock, he shrugged and let the boy keep them.

The time drifted past until the lights in the cell eventually dimmed, and once again Wanda drifted off into an uneasy sleep. The next day and the day after were exactly the same. Food was delivered to them at regular intervals, and a bathroom at the rear of the cell took care of their other necessities.

The hardest part was keeping the children occupied. Fortunately, Davy would play with his boxes for hours. In a desperate attempt to achieve some kind of normalcy, she started giving them lessons. The alien who had let Davy keep his boxes unexpectedly produced a chalklike marker for her to use. At first, Alicia didn't participate, but Wanda often found her watching them with an almost wistful expression. Eventually, she softened enough to volunteer a bedtime story. She proved to be a gifted storyteller and Wanda could see how eagerly the children, even Darla, listened to her tales.

"You're very good at that," Wanda murmured one evening after the lights dimmed and the children had fallen asleep.

"My grandmother used to tell me stories." The other woman's voice was unusually soft in the quiet cell.

"Is she... I mean, will she be worried?"

"No. I didn't leave anyone behind." Alicia turned her back, her voice cold once more.

After they had been on the ship for about a week, the glass wall opened again and a fifth person was thrust inside. Obviously of the same race as their captors, she was female and heavily pregnant at that.

"Perhaps this will teach you to obey," hissed the male who pushed her into the cell. "You need to remember that you're no better than they are."

The female sobbed as she collapsed onto the last empty bunk. Alicia and Wanda exchanged a look, but the older woman only shrugged and raised an eyebrow. Obviously it would be up to Wanda to make the first advance.

Cautiously, she went and sat down next to the newcomer. "Hi. My name is Wanda. What's your name?"

The female gave her a shocked look. Wanda realized she was quite young, her features softer than the other aliens.

"You wish to speak to me?" Her voice was almost too soft to hear.

"Well, yes. We're all in this cell together."

"But I'm Vedeckian. I'm one of the ones who took you."

"Are you responsible for the abductions?"

"No, but my—the captain is responsible."

"But that's not your fault. What's your name?"

"I'm Kareena." The other female managed a shy smile.

"When is your baby due?"

"Perhaps another month." More tears filled Kareena's eyes. "And then I'm going to lose her."

Kareena explained that children were a valuable commodity because of a plague called the Red Death that had swept through their civilization some years earlier. She had thought she would be allowed to keep her child, but when she had protested the treatment of the humans, the captain had made it clear that he had every intention of treating her the same way.

She didn't know if he would have left her with them until after the baby was born, but another week later, alarms started flashing outside their cell. Davy started to rock and protest, and Darla had to carry him when two guards appeared at the cell door and ordered them out. The Vedeckians marched them along a white corridor, through a cargo bay, and into a lifeboat.

It all happened so fast that Wanda hadn't even had a chance to protest or attempt to ask questions before the door was being slammed behind her. Kareena urged them all into the padded seats against the walls. She had just shown them how to fasten their harnesses when the lifeboat was jettisoned, tumbling out into space in a dizzying rush. When it finally stopped tumbling and the artificial gravity kicked in, the only thing they could see through the small portholes was empty space.

Unlike the larger ship, there were no periods of darkness to mark the days, and time had drifted by in a curious combination of boredom and terror. In many ways, it hadn't been that different from being in their cell, but at least they didn't have the constant threatening presence of the Vedeckians. The vessel had proven to be adequately stocked with food and water, and Kareena assured them that it would be emitting a beacon to notify any nearby ships.

And then Mganak had pulled them on to his ship and everything had changed again.

CHAPTER THREE

A fter a short trip to the bridge to set their destination, Mganak stalked down the corridor. He needed a session in the training room. His muscles were tense both from the presence of strangers on his ship and from fighting an urge to return to Wanda.

Was he doing the right thing? He could have done as she requested and sent them on their way, although he would have tried to contact the Patrol to come and pick them up. But even as he considered the idea, he dismissed it once again. Aside from the strange attraction that he—and his tail—seemed to have for the human female, he couldn't leave any of them alone and unprotected. He would take them to the nearest station at Ayuul and then they would be the responsibility of the Patrol. At least he knew they would be safe there, even though the idea of letting Wanda go already disturbed him.

As he passed the crew cabin, Sagat appeared in the doorway. The rajpar had long ago figured out how to operate the control panel next to the doors. Mganak peered through the door and saw that both children were asleep.

Good. It was probably for the best.

He closed the door and frowned at Sagat. "Are you ready to pay attention to me now?"

Sagat yawned, but then butted against Mganak's thigh. He winced at the heavy impact of the big head. "You will have to be careful with the children. They are not strong enough for that."

Sagat gave him an affronted look and stalked off, offended dignity in every line of his body. Mganak laughed and headed for the training room.

Half an hour later, he was dripping with sweat, his muscles aching. He had worked himself hard, but he obviously needed to put in more time in the training room. After he took a quick shower, he would see what kind of food he had on board that might be suitable for his visitors.

As he picked up his discarded uniform top, he heard a gasp and turned to find Wanda watching him, her eyes wide. A small pink tongue flicked out to trace those tantalizingly full lips as she studied him. His body responded as her gaze traveled across his chest and down the ridges of his abdomen to his suddenly fully engorged cock.

"Oh my," she whispered and he watched in fascination as a tide of pink swept up across her cheeks. She yanked her gaze away. "I... I'm sorry. I didn't mean to interrupt you."

"I was finished. I was just going to take a shower... That is, if you do not mind me using the sanitary facility in your cabin."

"No, no of course not. It's really your cabin."

"It is yours," he said firmly as the vision of her sprawled across his bed danced through his head. Would it ever feel like his cabin again? "But the other facilities are in the guest cabin and the crew quarters and I did not want to wake the children."

"I doubt Alicia would appreciate you coming through her

24

cabin either." She smiled and gave him a quick look, then murmured softly, "Or perhaps she would."

Her obvious appreciation was doing nothing to quell his unruly cock, but he did his best to ignore it. Despite his good intentions, he didn't pull his shirt back on. It would be foolish to get it dirty before he had a chance to take a shower, he told himself. The fact that she watched him so appreciatively had nothing to do with it.

"Were you looking for me?"

"Yes. I was wondering if I should bring some protein bars from the lifeboat."

He gave an exaggerated shudder. "I think I can provide something more edible than those."

"Are you sure? I don't want to take all of your supplies."

His tail curled around her back as he led her gently out of the training room. "I'm on my way back from a successful sale. I restocked while I was there. I have plenty of food."

She didn't protest, and she didn't move away from his tail just as she hadn't moved away from him as they stood in his cabin looking at the stars. This close to her, her sweet floral scent filled his head. He wanted to pull her closer to find out what was concealed under that flowing garment, to see if she tasted as wonderful as she smelled.

Sagat followed them out into the cargo hold, then curved his body around Wanda's legs. At first, she looked nervous, but when Sagat began to purr, she smiled and cautiously leaned forward to pat his head.

"He's so soft," she exclaimed. "I thought his scales would be rough."

"They can be. If he is threatened."

"He's beautiful. How long have you had him?"

"It is probably more appropriate to ask how long he has had me. I made a call in a port on Arslan. He was trapped in a cage, and I let him loose." An action that almost got him killed and ended up costing him most of his available credits. But he had never regretted it. "I assumed he would return to the wild. Instead, he followed me onto the ship and we have been together ever since."

She smiled a little wistfully. "That kind of loyalty is very rare."

"Is there no one who is loyal to you?"

"Not anymore. I was raised by a single father. He had an accident the year after I graduated from college, so I moved home to take care of him." She smiled again. "It wasn't exactly how I thought my life would turn out, but I think in the end it worked out for the best. I have—I had—a very happy life."

"Until the Vedeckians came for you," he said grimly.

"Yes. But hopefully your Patrol can take us all home again."

"Hopefully." He forced himself to agree with her even though he was already beginning to dread the prospect. The lights in the cargo hold were dim, and it created a sense of intimacy as they stood talking. That had to be what was creating these... unwanted feelings. He shook his head and firmly steered her towards the stairs.

"You will have to guide me as to what humans would like to eat."

She laughed. "We don't all like the same things."

"I still expect you will know more about your race's preferences than I will."

She threw a look over her shoulders as she took the first step, but her foot caught in her dress and she stumbled. He automatically reached out to catch her before she could fall and wound up with her body plastered against his. For a moment, he was distracted by the lush softness of her breasts against his bare chest but then he felt the firm mound of her stomach that had been concealed beneath her dress. His race might have lost their females, but he wasn't ignorant of the facts of reproduction. His whole body froze.

"You are mated?"

"Mated?" She sounded dazed, her body still leaning heavily against his.

"You are with child."

That fascinating tide of pink covered her cheeks again. "Yes, I am."

"Where is your mate? Was he left behind? He must be frantic."

"I don't have a mate. I'm doing this on my own."

"How is that possible?" His head spun at the notion. The Cire could not reproduce without a mating bond. Without it, their sperm would remain infertile.

She glared up at him and started to pull away. "I assure you it's quite possible. I don't need a man to have a child."

He belatedly realized that he had managed to offend her. "It is not physically possible amongst my people," he said quickly. "I meant no harm."

She studied his face, then nodded. "I'm sorry. I'm probably sensitive about it because a lot of people didn't understand why I would choose to have a baby by myself."

"You will have no one to take care of you." The thought horrified him. Even before the plague that killed all of the Cire females and destroyed the future of his race, a pregnant female was always nurtured and protected. But this brave human female was all alone.

"I told you. I can take care of myself." Her eyebrows drew together as she tried to pull back but only succeeded in wiggling against him. He bit back a groan at the indescribable pleasure of all that soft, warm flesh rubbing against him. His cock jerked and her eyes widened before she pushed more frantically against his arms. "And you can let me go now."

"No," he said firmly as he lifted her into his arms. "I will not take the chance of you falling on the stairs."

Ignoring her protest, he carried her up to the landing and immediately set her gently on her feet. "You should not take the stairs again. There is a cargo lift that you can use."

Her eyes blazed as she put her hands on her hips. The sight of her fiery defiance was even more arousing, but he forced himself to concentrate on her words.

"I'm not cargo," she fumed.

"No, of course not," he said hastily. "But you are with child and if anything should happen to you on my ship, I could never forgive myself. Please, Wanda. Do not take any chances."

She still looked ready to scratch his eyes out, but then Sagat butted his head gently against her hips and she gave a reluctant laugh. "Very well. I know when I'm outnumbered."

"Thank you." He bit back a sigh of relief.

She opened her mouth, then shook her head and headed for the galley.

"Kareena said that women and babies are very valuable," she said a minute later. "Is that why you're concerned?"

"My people have always revered their females, but I suppose now that they are gone all life is more precious."

"What do you mean? Gone?"

"Did the Vedeckian—"

"You mean Kareena," she interrupted.

"Did Kareena explain to you about the plague?"

"Yes, she said that it killed billions of people."

"It did. Most races suffered but the Cire were amongst the worst hit. We lost all of our females."

"All of them?"

"Yes. I had to watch my sister die. And then my father when he couldn't live with the guilt of having survived."

Her hand reached over and touched his arm, and his tail

came up to cover it. "I'm so sorry. Is that how you ended up here?"

"Yes. Our government tried artificial reproduction, and we were forced to contribute." Her hand tightened on his arm but he ignored it. "I hated it, so I stowed away on the first ship I could find."

"How old were you?"

"I had only just made the transition to manhood."

"What happened then?"

"The captain of the ship found me. Cursed me up one side and down the other, then wore his belt out on my backside."

"That's terrible."

He smiled at her indignation. "It probably was not as much as I deserved. And as soon as I learned my lesson, he took me on and taught me everything there was to know about running a ship. So here I am."

"What happened to the captain?"

"He is still around." The usual mixture of guilt and anger swept over him, but he shook his head. "Now enough about the past. What shall we cook?"

CHAPTER FOUR

As Wanda watched Mganak move around the ship's kitchen, she tried to sort out her mixed feelings. He had disappeared long enough to take a quick shower and returned wearing loose black pants and a shirt. But even though they concealed his body, she could still clearly visualize the intoxicating sight of his muscles rippling as he moved through his exercises. But it was more than just a physical attraction. Something about this alien called to her in a way she had never experienced before.

It's pointless to think about it, she scolded herself. He would take them to this Patrol and somehow they would find their way back to Earth. Although right now, her cozy cottage had never seemed as far away.

"What about jurj fruit?" he asked, presenting her with a misshapen orange blob. It didn't look remotely appealing, but then again, fruit would make a nice change.

"I don't know. What does it taste like?" She laughed as she realized the absurdity of the question. "I guess we don't really have any basis for comparison. Is it sweet?"

He regarded it a little doubtfully. "Not exactly. Here. I'll let you try it."

He deftly cut it open to reveal dark reddish flesh around a center stone, then handed her a small piece. She sniffed it cautiously and it had a faint, almost floral aroma. She took a cautious bite, and the taste exploded across her tongue, sweet and tart at the same time with a refreshing tang.

"Oh I like that."

He silently handed her the rest of the fruit, watching as she avidly consumed it, licking her fingers to get it all. Their eyes met as she sucked the last drop of juice from her fingers, and the tension flared between them. She could see the hunger in his eyes and felt an answering heat in her own body. Her breasts felt swollen and heavy, her nipples aching. Almost unconsciously, she started to reach for him...

"Davy's hungry." Darla's voice interrupted the moment, and she glared suspiciously from Wanda to Mganak. "What's going on?"

"I'm playing guinea pig to test out the food Mganak is preparing," Wanda said as calmly as possible, sure that she was blushing.

"Hmm." Darla looked skeptical but then she saw the remains of the fruit. Despite her attempt to maintain her disinterested air, Wanda saw her lick her lips. Even with the uninteresting wafers the Vedeckians had given them, the girl had managed to put on a little weight. She was still far too thin, in Wanda's opinion, but she no longer looked quite as waiflike as she had when she had first been abducted.

"Would you like to try one?"

Darla shook her head, despite a longing glance at the bowl of fruit. "I should go get Davy first."

"There is plenty for both of you," Mganak assured her.

She nodded and disappeared.

"She acts more like a mother than a sister," Mganak observed.

"Apparently their mother died while Davy was still very young. She's been watching out for her brother since not long after he was born. She's too young to have that much responsibility."

"It does her great honor."

"I know, but I wish she had the chance to be a child as well. I'm hoping that when we get back to Earth I can arrange to have both of them come and live with me."

"You would assume the care of two other children with a child on the way? Without a male to provide for you?"

She glared at him. "I already told you I don't need a male to provide for me."

"And I suspect that the young female would assure me that she does not need help either." Mganak frowned at her, then sighed and reached for her hand. "I mean no insult, mishka. I simply meant that it would be a difficult task with the approaching birth of your own child. But perhaps there are others who will help you?"

The question struck a nerve. She had lots of friends in town, and while she knew they would do what they could, they had their own lives and their own responsibilities. But she had known that when she made the decision to become a single parent. She forced a smile. "Yes," she said shortly.

From the way he was studying her face, she wasn't entirely sure that he believed her.

Darla reappeared, tugging Davy along behind her, and Mganak dropped the subject. Davy scowled suspiciously at the fruit. He was not a fan of anything new. But then Mganak showed him how to use the tool he had given him to cut the soft flesh into small cubes. After meticulously arranging the cubes by size, Davy actually ate his entire fruit.

In the meantime, Darla had consumed two more.

"Well, that was a success." Wanda smiled at him. "What's next on the menu?"

"I am making shol. It consists of meat and grain in a flavored broth."

The children wandered off to the seating area, and Sagat followed them. Wanda remained where she was, watching as Mganak assembled their meal. He moved with deft efficiency, appearing relaxed and at ease in the kitchen.

"You enjoy cooking?" she asked

"I enjoy eating." He flashed her a smile, and she realized it was the first time she had seen him look so carefree. "But yes, I also enjoy cooking. The ship has a replicator, of course, and a variety of prepared foods but whenever I am in port, I pick up fresh food. Do you like to cook?"

"I enjoy baking treats to take to the library for the children, but I'm guilty of picking up something fast and easy for most of my meals."

"The library?"

"That was my job." He nodded encouragingly, and she found herself telling him more about her life than she anticipated. He didn't say much, but he listened attentively and asked more questions whenever she paused. By the time the words ran down, the meal was ready and she felt oddly lighter. It had helped to talk about her old life and how much she had enjoyed it.

"Everything is ready," he said. "I will ask the other females to join us."

"Perhaps you'd better let me do that." She climbed a little awkwardly down from her stool. "Kareena is very shy."

He frowned but didn't say anything.

"Don't tell me you have a problem with her because she's a Vedeckian."

"No," he said slowly. "They do not have a good reputation, but I have never encountered any of their females before."

"She's a good person and has suffered just as much at their hands as we have."

He nodded but didn't look entirely convinced. She decided it wasn't worth arguing about. It would only take a short time in Kareena's company for him to realize how innocent she was.

When she knocked gently on the Vedeckian's door, she found the other woman sitting perfectly still in the middle of her small bed.

"Mganak has prepared a meal for us," Wanda said cheerfully. "It will be a nice change from protein bars."

Kareena nodded but didn't get up.

"Aren't you going to join us?"

"It is allowed?"

"Of course it is. Why would you think anything else?"

Kareena raised a shoulder in a slight shrug. "My people are not often welcome."

"Well you are welcome and you need to eat. You have to think about your baby."

A wistful smile curved Kareena's lips as she rose to her feet with an enviable amount of grace. "I do think about her. All the time. I just hope I get to keep her."

Wanda's heart ached but she forced herself to smile. "I'm sure this Patrol won't let anyone take your baby away."

"Perhaps. They don't think much of Vedeckians either."

"Then we'll just have to convince them that you're different," she said firmly. "The lounge is at the end of the hall. I'm going to get Alicia and then I'll join you."

Kareena gave her a shaky smile and walked away while Wanda knocked on Alicia's door. There was no immediate response, and she had just decided that maybe the other woman was sleeping when the door opened.

"Mganak has prepared a meal for us."

"I hope it's edible," Alicia sniffed.

Wanda felt a rush of annoyance. "Why do you have to be like that? He's just trying to do something nice."

Alicia drew herself up, and Wanda braced for a withering comment, but then the other woman sagged unexpectedly. "I'm sorry. You're right. It's just..."

"It's just what?" Wanda asked gently.

Alicia looked at her, and for the first time Wanda noticed the faint traces that indicated the normally unflappable woman had been crying.

"It all feels so futile, somehow. Even if they manage to take us back, we're not the same anymore. I'm not the same. I could never tell anyone about this." Alicia's lips twisted bitterly. "Everyone would think I was crazy."

"Not everyone. I know you aren't crazy."

She hadn't really considered the matter before, but Alicia was right. They would never be able to tell anyone. How was she ever going to explain her absence to the library board? What if she lost her job? Firmly putting that horrible thought aside to deal with at another time, she reached out and gave Alicia's hand a quick squeeze.

"We'll think of something. And if you ever want to talk about it, you can come visit me."

"In the charming city of Edgerton?" Despite the slightly sardonic question, Alicia's smile was genuine as she returned the clasp of Wanda's hand. "All right. Let's go try your captain's cooking."

Wanda felt the heat rising in her cheeks. "He's not my captain."

"Isn't he?" Alicia arched a knowing eyebrow before heading to the lounge.

Wanda followed, her cheeks still burning, but when she entered the room and saw Mganak waiting for her, she couldn't help a feeling of regret. Under other circumstances, she thought perhaps he could have been her captain.

CHAPTER FIVE

A subdued group sat around the table to eat the meal that Mganak had prepared. It had an odd resemblance to chicken and rice soup, although it couldn't possibly have been either chicken or rice. Nonetheless, it was warm and comforting, and everyone devoured it eagerly, along with a loaf of hard, reddish bread with a pleasant nutty taste. Davy wouldn't eat the soup, but he ate more fruit after once again cutting it into small cubes. He also accepted the bread readily enough.

No one had much to say, and Wanda suspected that they were all still stunned at the change in circumstances. Could they actually be on the first step of the journey home? Alicia's questions rang through her mind. How were they going to be able to explain their absence? If her calculations were correct and it had taken them three weeks to get to this point, would it be another three weeks before they were home? And how could she explain the six-week absence?

Kareena excused herself as soon as the meal was finished. She had eaten quickly and quietly, casting nervous glances at Mganak as she did. Wanda wanted to reassure her, but she suspected that only time would ease the other female's nervousness. Considering that her own people had decided to use her for breeding, Wanda could understand her hesitation.

To Wanda's surprise, Alicia offered to help clean up after dinner but Mganak shook his head. "The galley is too small for more than one person and I know where everything should go."

"Very well." Alicia nodded regally, then cast a quick, wistful glance at the children.

"Is your ship set for a night shift?" Wanda asked Mganak quietly.

"It is. And it will occur quite shortly, unless that displeases you."

"Not at all. I think we're all tired. The lifeboat didn't track time, and that seemed to make it harder to maintain any kind of schedule." She turned to Alicia. "Perhaps you could tell the children a story before they go to bed."

Darla immediately scowled at both of them. "It's too early to go to bed. I'm not tired."

"You were sleeping earlier," Wanda said dryly.

"Which is why I'm not tired now." The words would have been more convincing if they hadn't been interrupted by a huge yawn. Darla rolled her eyes, then gave a sheepish grin. "All right, all right. But we're gonna talk about this tomorrow."

Wanda gave her a quick, affectionate hug. "Whatever you say, sweetheart."

"Come on, Davy." Oblivious to their conversation, her brother had taken the last of the bread and started arranging it in a pattern on the tabletop. "Time for bed. Miss Alicia is going to tell us the story."

He screwed up his face, and Wanda held her breath, wondering if this was the onset of another meltdown.

"Sagat too," he insisted. The animal was curled under the table, but he lifted his head when Davy said his name.

Mganak laughed. "He goes where he wants to go, but he likes to find a comfortable spot and he seems to like your bunk. Perhaps he will join you."

Davy climbed down from the table and poked his head under the table. "Sleep here."

"Why don't we try your bunk first?" Wanda suggested.

To her relief, when Davy reluctantly agreed, Sagat stretched and accompanied him out of the room.

Which meant that she and Mganak were alone. The awareness of his presence that had been building since their earlier encounter flared up again. Rather than look at him, she began gathering up the dishes. "Do you have a dishwasher?"

"A machine to clean with? Yes, but you do not need to do anything else."

"I'll just carry these into the galley," she said quickly.

"You do not need to help me. You should be resting."

"I've done nothing but rest," she huffed as she carried the dishes into the small kitchen area. "I probably need some exercise."

She turned as she finished talking and realized that he was right behind her. Big and green and muscled, and close enough that she could feel the heat emanating from his body and catch that wonderful, tantalizing fragrance. The kitchen suddenly seemed to shrink around them until the two of them were locked in their own little bubble.

"If you would really like to exercise, I would be happy to assist."

His voice was low and husky, and she had a sudden vision of what that exercise might entail. A pulse of arousal rushed to her suddenly swollen clit. How long had it been since she had been with a man? The disadvantage of small towns was that everyone knew your business, and she preferred to keep some things to herself. As a result, it had been almost two years since she ended an amiable but ultimately unsatisfying relationship with a lawyer in Charleston.

It's just hormones, she told herself firmly. *The books all mentioned that my libido might increase later in my pregnancy.* But this didn't feel like hormones—this felt deeper and more urgent.

He was still waiting for a reply, she realized with a start and gave a nervous laugh. "Maybe some other time. It's been kind of a long day. At least I think it's been a day. Time is all muddled up in my head."

"We will be sure and keep it straight from now on." He raised his hand and gently touched her cheek, his fingers warm and slightly rough. "You should go to bed, mishka."

She nodded but couldn't quite force herself to move. "What does that mean? Mishka? You called me that earlier."

"It is a term of... affection amongst my people."

"Oh. That's nice." She couldn't look away from him, her gaze resting on his mouth. His lips were thin, almost nonexistent. What would they feel like against her own?

He growled suddenly, a low, hungry noise that sent another pulse of desire through her body. Before she could respond, he removed the dishes she was still holding from her hands and somehow maneuvered her back towards the entrance. In the process, their bodies touched, and she almost moaned when her aching nipples rubbed against the firm muscles of his chest.

"Bed," he repeated. "Before I forget my good intentions."

"Bed." She nodded and headed for the stairs, feeling dazed by their close encounter. Just as she reached the bottom step, a pair of strong arms lifted her effortlessly against his chest.

"I apologize. I forgot that you needed assistance."

"I really don't," she protested weakly, but there was something extraordinarily comforting about having him carry her.

"There is no need to take chances." He climbed the stairs

easily, but with no great speed, and when he reached the top and let her slide down his body, he seemed as reluctant to let her go as she felt.

"Um. Thank you. I'll see you in the morning."

"I will look forward to it."

They stared at each other a moment longer, and then she forced herself to turn away.

"Feel free to make use of my clothing if you would like to change," he called after her.

"Thank you," she repeated. She didn't turn back, afraid that if she saw him watching her, she would give into the urge to throw herself back into his arms. What on earth was wrong with her?

"Sleep well, mishka." The words echoed after her as she closed the cabin door.

Once again, she was drawn to the wide vista of stars surrounding the ship. They shimmered now, flowing past as the ship traveled deeper into the unknown. Everything about this experience was unknown—except the feelings that Mganak aroused, even if she had never encountered that intensity before.

Finally, she sighed and went to explore the small bathroom. The fixtures were very similar to those on the Vedeckian ship but there was one important difference. Here she didn't feel afraid.

During their time in captivity, she usually showered with her clothes on, both as a way to clean them and because she hated the vulnerability of being naked and a prisoner. Now when she stripped off everything and stepped under the stream of warm water, it hit her with an unexpectedly sensual pleasure.

Soaping her hands, she ran them over her breasts, larger and more sensitive than ever before. She shivered with pleasure but couldn't help imagining Mganak's hands holding her instead. Her body ached with frustrated desire, and she slipped her hand between her legs, stroking herself to a rapid climax as she envisioned Mganak watching her and urging her on.

Afterwards, her body felt loose and relaxed, and she sleepily pulled one of his shirts over her head. It smelled like him, as did the sheets when she crawled into his bed. It was almost like being wrapped in his arms and with that thought comforting her, she slipped into a deep, peaceful sleep.

Mganak stood on the landing, fighting the urge to go after Wanda. He was sure she was experiencing the same attraction he felt. The sweet scent of her arousal had made his head swim, and the lingering memory of her hard little nipples rubbing against his chest made his cock jerk. His tail lashed anxiously, trying to reach for the door panel.

Since leaving Ciresia, he'd had a few encounters with females but they had all been unsatisfying. In order to achieve full release, a Cire male needed to knot inside his mated female. Since there were no more Cire females with whom to mate, he had assumed that he would never achieve that release. And yet, lately he had heard rumors that a Cire male could mate with a female from another species.

But even if that were true, Wanda was not for him. She wished to return to her planet to give birth and he could understand her urge to return home. Even if she wished to stay, what did he have to offer her other than a ship and an uncertain future as a salvage operator. His life had suited him, but it was not the life for a mated male.

He had chosen this way of life, and until now, he had never had reason to doubt his choice. He had long ago accepted the loneliness, and after that final argument with Rafalo, he had no bonds to tie him to anything other than the ship. It would be foolish to consider any other future.

Nonetheless, the thought kept intruding as he returned to the galley and finished cleaning. He checked on the children and found Sagat keeping guard over them. He raised his head when Mganak cracked open the door, then settled back down. The young male was pressed against his side, and Mganak knew that no harm would come to either child while Sagat was present.

He didn't disturb the other two females although he heard restless movements from the medical lab and thought he detected the sound of quiet weeping from the other cabin. He felt sorrow for the two females, but the best he could offer them was to get them to Ayuul and hope that the Patrol would be able to find their homes.

As he started to head for the training room, he hesitated. What if Wanda needed something in the night? He would be too far away to get to her quickly. And what if she attempted the stairs on her own?

That thought decided him. He would spend the night in the pilot's chair. It might not be the most comfortable sleep he had ever had but he would be nearby in case she needed him and that was far more important.

When he reached the landing, he caught the hint of her arousal in the lingering dampness from her shower. How he wished he had been there to satisfy her. His cock throbbed in urgent agreement. It was going to be a long night.

CHAPTER SIX

W anda drifted reluctantly awake, snuggling deeper into the warm and deliciously fragrant sheets. She actually felt rested, and she realized that she had slept soundly all night long. Although she was tempted by the idea of going back to sleep, her bladder was making its presence known—definitely one of the downsides of pregnancy.

Her morning needs attended to, she started to pick up her dress and then decided she really couldn't stand the idea of yet another day in the same clothes. The shirt she had borrowed from Mganak did a more than adequate job of covering her—it reached almost to her knees, and she'd had to roll the sleeves up many times to get her hands free. At least it was something different.

Although she searched the bathroom, there was nothing resembling a comb. She ended up finger combing her hair and fastening it back in a rough braid again. There also no mirror to check her appearance, but there was no one she needed to impress, she told herself firmly. It was pointless to dream of dazzling Mganak with a fancy hairdo and a sexy outfit.

Not that I want to dazzle him.

Last night must have been a fluke, brought on by tiredness and relief that perhaps she was finally on the way home. Today she would keep her distance from the big, sexy alien.

That resolve disappeared as soon as she opened the door and looked across at the bridge. Mganak was sprawled in one of the chairs, his feet up on the other. He was asleep, and she let herself look at him, her gaze traveling down over the strangely attractive features to the broad chest and then down his body. Her eyes snagged on the massive outline of his cock straining against the tight black pants. *Oh my.* Was he erect all the time, or was it possible that he grew even larger?

A shiver of what she tried to tell herself was trepidation worked its way down her spine. Would she be able to take him? Not that it was going to occur, of course.

"Good morning, mishka."

The sound of his deep voice made her jump, and she yanked her eyes back up to his face to find him watching her, clearly amused.

"I'm sorry. I didn't mean to wake you."

He shook his head as he swung his feet to the ground, then stretched. The move made his muscles ripple intriguingly beneath the loose shirt.

"You didn't wake me. The chairs are not as comfortable as I had hoped."

"I thought you were going to sleep in the training room."

With a final stretch, he stood and came to her, his tail immediately curling around her waist. "I didn't want to be that far away in case you needed something in the night."

Any hope of maintaining distance between them melted.

Who would have thought that such a big, rough warrior would be so sweet?

"It really isn't necessary." Her voice came out low and breathless, and somehow she was leaning up against him.

He kept his eyes on her face, and for a moment she thought he was going to kiss her, but then Darla's voice sounded from below.

"Wanda! Are you up there? Where is everybody?"

She could hear the uncertainty in the girl's voice and immediately felt guilty for not remembering the children might be anxious. "I'm here. I'll be right down."

As soon as she finished speaking, Mganak lifted her into his arms and started carrying her down the stairs.

"I keep telling you that I can walk down the stairs. And your shirt is short enough that I'm not going to trip over it. I hope you don't mind me borrowing it."

"Not at all." His heated gaze swept down over the open collar to her bare calves. "It has never looked better."

Warmth filled her cheeks, and she knew that she was still blushing when they reached the bottom and he placed her on her feet. Darla glared at her.

"How come you got something new to wear?"

"I—" More guilt filled her at the realization that everyone was as tired of their clothes as she was.

"I offered her the use of my wardrobe," Mganak interrupted. "I don't have much variety, but I'm willing to share with all of you."

"Really?" Darla's excitement made her look even younger than usual. "I'm so ready for something different."

"Yes, as long as you don't take everything." Mganak smiled at the girl, and she grinned back.

"Maybe we can leave you one or two things."

"What do you say, Darla?" Wanda prompted.

"Thank you. I really mean that. Can I go look now?"

"Where's Davy?"

A guilty look crossed Darla's face. "He's cutting up fruit again. I figured at least it would encourage him to eat it, but I should probably stop him before he goes through all of it."

"Do not worry," Mganak assured her. "I have plenty."

The three of them trooped into the lounge, then Mganak went to check on Davy. He somehow persuaded the boy to distribute the carefully sized cubes into bowls for breakfast. While Mganak was adding some type of grain to the breakfast bowls, Alicia came to join them.

Her gaze swept over Wanda's attire and although she didn't say anything, her raised eyebrow was remarkably eloquent.

"Mganak has offered to share his clothing with us," Wanda said defensively, sure that she was blushing again.

A flash of longing crossed Alicia's face. "It would be nice to have a change."

"You are all welcome to choose something, although I do not have much variety," Mganak offered. "And I'm afraid they will not fit well."

"I can see that," Alicia said sardonically, then winced. "I'm sorry. I shouldn't have said that. If you have any sewing tools, perhaps I could do some tailoring."

"You know how to sew?" Wanda couldn't hide her astonishment, and a tinge of color tinted Alicia's dusky cheeks.

"I grew up poor. If I wanted something, I had to learn to make it."

"That would certainly come in handy. It's never been one of my skills," Wanda admitted, deciding not to pursue the subject of Alicia's childhood poverty. For some reason, she had assumed the other woman had always been as wealthy as she appeared to be now. "I'll just go get—"

Kareena appeared at the entrance to the lounge before she finished speaking, hovering shyly in the opening.

Wanda smiled at her. "Good, there you are. It looks like breakfast is ready."

Davy was carefully carrying the bowls to the table, arranging them in a neat line, and they all sat down together. The tension of the previous day had dissipated and it felt oddly homelike. Wanda smiled as she picked up her spoon.

AFTER BREAKFAST, THE FEMALES RAIDED HIS WARDROBE. Mganak bit back a sigh and let them choose whatever they wanted. Although he did not begrudge them the use of his clothing, he would have preferred to limit it to Wanda. It didn't seem quite right on anyone else.

The older female proved to be quite adept with the cutting and seaming tools he procured for her, and the lounge was soon a sea of fabric.

"I have some work to do," he murmured to Wanda.

She gave him a grateful look. "I'm sorry. I know we've kind of taken over."

"My ship is your ship," he said softly.

"At least until we get to Ayuul." Her smile looked forced, but he couldn't dispute her answer. As he turned away, a small hand tugged on his pants, and he looked down to find the young male staring up at him.

"Davy help."

"No!" Darla came rushing over. "Davy, you need to stay here with me."

The boy scowled and began to shake his head. "No. No. No."

"He will be quite safe with me. I promise you. And with Sagat."

The rajpar had appeared at the first sound of the boy's distress and now he leaned against him, purring. The boy's restless movements ceased and after a moment, Darla sighed.

"If anything happens to him, I'll find a way to hurt you," she said fiercely.

"I will guard his safety with my life," he vowed.

Wanda approached and put her arm around the young female's thin shoulders. "Mganak will take care of him. Now come with me," she coaxed. "Alicia wants to know how long to make the sleeves."

With a last scowl at Mganak, the girl let Wanda pull her away.

"Now, my young helper, shall we leave the females to their sewing?"

Davy nodded and marched ahead of him down the corridor. He was fascinated by Mganak's workshop and wanted to touch everything at first. Mganak finally gave him a container full of assorted screws, and the boy happily sat and sorted them by size. Once he was finished, he mixed them together and started all over again. He seemed quite content and only reacted poorly once, when Mganak turned on a drill. At the first whine of the machinery, he began to rock and protest. Mganak immediately turned it off and Sagat pressed against Davy, purring loudly, until he calmed.

About an hour later, Darla poked her head around the entrance to the workshop. She was wearing a simple black tunic and pants. She seemed very happy with the new outfit, twirling in front of him. "Look what Alicia made me!"

"It looks very nice," he said truthfully. The outfit fit her well but he regretted he didn't have something more colorful for her to wear.

"What are you doing?"

"I am cleaning filters," he said as he scrubbed another one. "Unfortunately, it is a never-ending job."

"What kind of filters?"

"They cleanse the air and the water on board the ship. But they have to be cleansed as well. Frequently."

She watched him for a few minutes. "Can I help?"

"Are you through with sewing?"

She shrugged. "I got bored. I would rather help you."

"All right. But you have to be very careful."

He showed her how to use the sonic brush, then pass the filters through the cleansing bath. She watched him intently, then took the next one. When she handed it back to him, he inspected it carefully, but to his surprise, it was as pristine as if he had done the work himself.

"This is excellent. You did very well."

Her whole face glowed. "I really did a good job?"

"I could not have done a better one. Would you like to do another?"

She nodded eagerly and he let her take over cleaning the filters while he started mending a replicator. As they worked, she started to ask him about the various dismantled machines surrounding them, at first shyly, but when he responded willingly to her questions, her enthusiasm grew. She had a quick mind and an aptitude for understanding how things came together.

They were deep in a discussion about the workings of the water purifier when Wanda appeared in the doorway. All thoughts of water purification disappeared. She was still wearing one of his shirts but it had been cut to fit the curvy lines of her body, accentuating the ripe bounty of her breasts and the firm swell of her stomach. All of the blood in his body rushed to his cock so quickly that he felt dizzy.

"I came to see if anyone wanted some lunch," she said with

a rueful smile. "Although I freely admit that it is not up to your standards."

Darla jumped down from where she had been sitting cross-legged next to him. "I'm hungry. Come on, Davy."

Her brother hesitated, frowning down at the pile of screws.

"You can sort them again later," he promised and Sagat nudged the boy towards the door.

The children vanished, leaving him alone with Wanda. Unable to resist, he moved towards her, prowling with the determination of one of his ancient ancestors.

"You look beautiful, mishka." The pink flooded her cheeks again, but she didn't back away, not even when his tail tugged her up against his body. The scent of her arousal perfumed the air and he could feel the hard points of her nipples against his chest.

"I'm glad you like it. We tried to make sure you had at least a few things left." Her voice sounded breathless again and she was staring at his mouth.

"You are welcome to everything I have." The words rang with unexpected clarity in the quiet room, and he recognized the truth of them as he spoke. How was he ever going to let this female go?

"Do you... That is, do your people kiss?" she asked shyly.

The word did not seem to translate correctly.

"Press our mouths together? Why would we do that?"

"For pleasure." The color on her cheeks deepened, but she raised a small hand and tugged his head down towards hers.

He went willingly enough, but he was unsure of her intentions. Her mouth brushed against his, impossibly soft. It was a pleasant sensation, but he still didn't understand why she wished to touch him in such a way. But then her soft little tongue entered his mouth. By Granthar's Hammer! Her delicious taste exploded in his mouth and the silky feel of her tongue shyly exploring his sent streaks of pleasure down his spine. Desperate for more, he cupped her head, holding her in place as he explored her mouth with frantic urgency.

He wanted more, needed more, and he lifted her into his arms so that her soft, luscious body was pressed against his. She moaned, and he hesitated for a moment, but then her arms tightened around his neck and she wiggled frantically against him. He could feel the damp heat of her naked cunt rubbing against his stomach and he grasped the soft curve of her buttock, pressing her more firmly against him. He was seconds away from sliding her down onto his aching cock before he came to his senses and finally raised his head.

Her eyes opened slowly, her face dazed, her mouth pink and swollen and utterly tempting.

"For someone who didn't understand kissing, you sure learned in a hurry," she murmured, then the color washed over her cheeks again as she pushed lightly at his shoulders. "Can you put me down?"

Even though he was appalled by his behavior, he still had to force himself to place her on her feet once more. "Should I apologize?"

"Oh no. No. I was a very willing participant." Small white teeth closed over that swollen lower lip. "But... we probably shouldn't. We're going back to Earth, and you're going back into space."

A prospect that had never seemed less appealing, but he nodded. "I understand. We should join the others."

As they left the workshop, he frowned at her. "How did you get down here?"

"Don't worry. I took the lift—even though I don't think it's necessary." He started to reach for her, and she added hastily, "Maybe we should take it back up as well."

The fact that he was already anticipating having her in his

arms again argued that her suggestion was correct, but it didn't make his chest ache any less as he silently led the way to the lift.

Both of them were subdued during the meal, but the others didn't seem to notice. Alicia and Kareena discussed clothing with surprising enthusiasm. The Vedeckian female was more animated than he had ever seen her. Darla seemed just as thrilled to explain how she had been helping him.

Afterwards, he returned to the shop alone, despite the protests from both children.

"I need to use the drill and the noise bothers Davy," he explained.

Darla scowled at him. "It doesn't bother me."

"We should spend some time on your lessons," Wanda interjected.

"Why? Machines are much more interesting."

"But it is helpful to understand how they work," he said firmly. "An education is important."

Darla rolled her eyes, but she went to join her brother without any further protest.

"Thank you." Wanda sighed. "She's very bright. I wish I had more resources to keep her interested."

"I will look tonight and see if I have anything you can use." He looked down at her and realized that his tail was stroking her arm. "I will miss you this afternoon."

"I... I..."

She looked up at him helplessly, and he made himself change the subject. "And I will be in charge of the evening meal."

She looked startled, then laughed. "I told you I wasn't a very good cook."

"Then it is just as well that I am happy to cook for you."

With a last lingering stroke of her arm, he pulled his reluctant tail away and went back to his workshop. He spent most of his time there during his trips and he'd always found a quiet satisfaction in repairing machines and making them functional again. Today that satisfaction was strangely absent. He missed the sound of Davy busily sorting parts, he missed Darla's eager questions, and most of all, he missed the warmth of Wanda's presence.

CHAPTER SEVEN

Wanda watched Mganak depart with a wistful smile. Was he already tired of them? He must be used to being alone. Maybe he needed a breather. Trying her best not to think about his absence, she turned her attention to the children.

But Mganak did not stay away for long. She was working with Davy on a simple counting game when he reappeared.

"Are you through with your work?" she asked.

"There is always work to be done." He shrugged. "I missed my helpers."

He dropped a casual hand on Darla's thin shoulder, and the girl beamed up at him. "I can come help you now."

"Are you finished with your lessons?"

"Kind of." When he raised an eyebrow, she pouted. "It's boring."

"Darla is not a fan of history," Wanda said dryly.

"But if you do not understand history, how do you prevent yourself from making the same mistake?"

Wanda laughed. "We have a similar expression. But I

suspect that science lessons might be more to her taste. Unfortunately, it's not really my strong point." She shot him a challenging look. "Do you want to try?"

To her surprise, he didn't immediately reject the idea. After rubbing his chin for a moment, he retrieved a tablet and started scrolling through it rapidly before offering it to Darla. "Here. This is one of the first manuals that Rafalo gave me to study. I know you do not understand the language, but there are a number of diagrams."

Darla gave him a suspicious look, but she reached for the tablet anyway. Almost immediately, she looked up and grinned at him. "Isn't this the water purifier we were talking about?"

Mganak beamed proudly. "It is indeed. Remember that we were discussing filtration?"

The two heads bent over the tablet as Wanda suppressed a smile and turned back to Davy. He played the game one more time, then scowled and shoved all of the pieces to the floor. Darla gave him an anxious look, but then Sagat curled around Davy's ankles. His frustration seemed to dissipate, but Wanda noticed that he still seemed unsettled.

Leaving both children with Mganak, she went to Alicia's cabin to try on another outfit. Once Alicia made a few notations, the two of them chatted for a few minutes.

"You know, I married young." Alicia's lips curved in a reminiscent smile as Wanda shot her a surprised look. The other woman had not been particularly forthcoming about her past. "Thomas was smart, ambitious. Good looking. We knew what we wanted out of life and we got it. He had a successful practice and we had the big house, the social status that we both wanted."

"Children?" Wanda asked tentatively.

Alicia shook her head. "At first, we didn't have time. He had to get through medical school and then set up the practice.

When we finally decided to try, it never happened for us." She looked away, her eyes distant. "My fault, as it turned out. We should have adopted—Thomas wouldn't have objected—but by then I was caught up in this illusion of a perfect life, and it was easier to pretend that we had decided against having children."

"You would have been a wonderful mother," Wanda said sincerely.

"Would I?" Alicia's face was still distant. "I was so sure of how everything should be. I suspect I would have driven the children away."

"You haven't driven Davy and Darla away."

"I'm very happy about that. But I suspect it's because I have changed. First I lost Thomas. All those plans we had to travel, to enjoy our retirement, gone. And now this." She waved a hand. "It tends to give you a new perspective."

"That's one way of putting it." Wanda laughed and started to stand up. To her surprise, Alicia reached out and took her hand.

"What I'm trying to say—not very eloquently—is that you should seize happiness where you find it. Don't put it off waiting for the perfect time. Grab it while you can."

Wanda bit her lip. "I'm not sure I understand."

"Oh, I think you do. Let your captain make you happy, even if it's just for now."

She knew she was blushing again as she mumbled something incoherent. Alicia shook her head and released her hand.

"Perhaps I am still too sure about everything."

"I... Thank you." She bent down and gave the older woman a quick hug. Alicia stiffened, then awkwardly patted her back.

"I'll just go help Mganak with dinner," Wanda said as she drew back.

"I hope your definition of help means that you are going to

sit there and watch him cook," Alicia said in her familiar sardonic tone, but her eyes were smiling.

"We'll see. Maybe I can convince him to experiment," she teased.

"Heaven help us all."

After they ate, Davy begrudgingly agreed to go to bed although Wanda suspected it was only because Sagat accompanied him. To the older woman's obvious pleasure, he also insisted that Alicia tell him a bedtime story.

Tonight, Wanda didn't try and make Darla accompany him. Instead, Mganak and Darla spent more time poring over the manual while Alicia and Kareena did some more sewing.

Wanda had decided to try and reproduce one of her craft projects from the library. During her rather unfortunate attempt to fix lunch, she had discovered that the juice of several of the fruits and vegetables Mganak had on the ship caused stains on fabric. She used them now to die some thin strips of cord that Mganak had provided her. She was just checking to see if they were dry when Darla wandered over.

"Whatcha doing?"

"Dying this string." She held up the bright red and orange strands. "I thought I would try making a bracelet."

She had too much experience with teenagers to suggest that Darla make one. Instead, she started fumbling with the strips until the girl gave an exaggerated sigh and reached for them. "Why don't you let me try?"

By the time the ship lights started to dim, Darla had created woven bracelets for all of them, including Mganak. He nodded gravely when she tied it around his wrist. "I am honored."

Darla blushed, threw her arms around his waist in a quick hug, flushed even darker, then disappeared down the corridor with a muttered goodnight.

"You're very good with her," Wanda said softly.

"I enjoy her companionship." He rubbed his face thoughtfully. "One of the programs on the tablet is designed to teach reading. Do you think she would enjoy that?"

A pang of longing shot through Wanda. How much she missed reading. "I think she would, even if it's just so that she can understand that manual. But I would like to learn as well. Perhaps after she's in bed?"

"Of course." His tail curved gently around her wrist. "I would have suggested it before but I know that you are returning to your planet."

He sounded as though he were forcing himself to remember, and she was shocked to realize that she hadn't been considering the short time remaining either. She made herself smile and say lightly, "Learning is never a waste of time."

"No," he agreed, his eyes focused on her face. She was suddenly extremely conscious of the fact that they were alone again in a dimly lit room. When he bent towards her, she held her breath, expecting him to kiss her. Instead, he lifted her easily into his arms as he headed for the upper stairs. "Time for bed."

Such an innocent remark and yet her head was immediately filled with images of Mganak sharing that big bed with her, of holding her even more tightly against his muscular body, of his face rising over her as he entered her. Her whole body was taut with desire, and when they reached the landing and he let her slide to the ground, the massive bar of his cock made it clear that he was equally aroused.

Alicia's words flitted through her head, and she started to sway towards him when a fluttering sensation in her stomach made her jump.

"Is something wrong?"

"Not at all." She grabbed his hand eagerly and placed it on

her stomach. "I just felt the baby move. I thought I did once or twice before but was never sure. This time, I'm sure."

He waited patiently, his big hand warm on her stomach, and just as she was about to give up, she felt it again. Awe filled Mganak's face.

"I felt that. I felt your child."

Her eyes filled with unexpected tears. Part of her was overjoyed that he had been here to experience this moment, but it reminded her of what was at stake. She couldn't—wouldn't—allow herself to be sidetracked by her attraction to Mganak. She had to concentrate on getting her baby back to Earth. The moment had passed, and she stepped back with a shaky smile.

"Good night, Mganak."

"Good night, mishka." His face was grave, but he didn't protest, and she wondered if he was experiencing the same doubts.

She gave him another quick smile and darted into the cabin but she found it impossible to put him out of her mind as she went about getting ready for bed. Had he thought she was rejecting him? Did he understand why she was so conflicted? Maybe she should just talk to him.

Before she could change her mind, she opened the cabin door and then her heart melted completely. Once again he was sprawled uncomfortably in the pilot's chair and she knew it was only so that he could be there in case she needed him.

"This is ridiculous," she said firmly. "That bed is big enough for both of us."

"Are you sure?" He prowled over to her with a predatory grace that sent an answering streak of excitement down her spine.

"To sleep," she added quickly, shocked at how seductive her voice sounded. "I... I'm very attracted to you, Mganak, but I have to return to Earth. My daughter deserves to grow up on her own planet."

"I understand, mishka. It will be... difficult for me to let you go, and it would be even harder if there was more between us."

Her chest aching, she nodded. "But the offer still stands. If you would like to share the bed...?"

He smiled and it only looked a little forced. "I would appreciate a full night's sleep."

As she turned to lead the way into the cabin, hoping she wasn't making a mistake, Darla came rushing up the stairs, her face frantic.

"Davy is having a meltdown and I can't get him calm. Can you help me?"

"Of course we will." Mganak had Wanda up in his arms as he spoke, heading for the stairs. "What does he need?"

"I... I don't know." Darla's face was a combination of worry and defiance. "Sometimes he just gets like this. But he doesn't mean it," she added hastily.

"We know that, sweetheart," Wanda said reassuringly.

As soon as they reached the lower level, they could hear Davy screeching. Alicia and Kareena were both standing outside the cabin door, identical looks of concern on their faces.

"I don't know what to do," Alicia said, wringing her hands. "I offered to tell him some more stories, but it's like he doesn't even hear me."

Inside the cabin, Davy was marching back and forth from wall to wall, still screeching. No words were discernible, only harsh sounds that hit Wanda like nails on a chalkboard. Sagat prowled back and forth in step with the boy, his tail lashing, but Davy seemed oblivious to the rajpar and didn't stop long enough for Sagat to press up against him.

Mganak entered the cabin, kneeling down so that he was at the boy's eye level just as he had done when they met. This time, Davy ignored him even when Mganak tried to distract him with the multitool. Mganak gave Wanda a worried glance, his tail lashing almost as furiously as Sagat's.

"Darla, is there anything we can do for him?" Wanda asked softly.

The girl shook her head, her eyes filled with tears. "Not when he gets like this. I just have to wait with him."

Despite Darla's determined words, Wanda could see how desperate the girl looked. How often over the years had she had to take care of her brother when he was like this? Did anyone ever take care of her?

"Not tonight," she said firmly. She darted a quick look at Alicia and the other woman nodded. "You go with Alicia and I will stay with him."

"*We* will stay with him," Mganak interjected.

"But he's my brother. He's my responsibility."

"I know he's your brother, sweetheart, but you can trust us to look after him. You need to get some rest so you can be there for him tomorrow."

Darla hesitated, clearly torn, and Alicia put her careful arm around those thin shoulders. "Come on, honey. Everything is going to be fine."

With a final worried look at her brother, Darla followed Alicia across the hall and into her cabin.

"Is there anything I can do to help?" Kareena said softly.

"I don't think so. You need to rest as well."

"All right." The Vedeckian hesitated. "If you would allow me the use of your galley, Captain Mganak, I thought perhaps the girl would like a hot drink. I could make shoko."

Mganak nodded approvingly. "An excellent idea. Please feel free to help yourself to any of the supplies."

A faint hint of color touched Kareena's cheekbones before she nodded and disappeared down the corridor.

"Shoko?" Wanda asked.

"It is a drink often given to children that is both sweet and soothing."

"That sounds nice," she said wistfully, but she had more important things to worry about right now. Davy was still marching back and forth, although the sounds he was making had diminished a little. Sagat continued to keep pace with him. Wanda settled down next to Mganak to keep watch.

When Kareena reappeared a few minutes later, she shyly offered them both a mug of shoko. Mganak refused with a smile, but Wanda took it gratefully.

"This is so good," she groaned as she took a sip. It bore a distinct resemblance to hot chocolate, although with a nuttier taste.

Kareena gave her a pleased smile and insisted on leaving the second mug. Wanda heard her take two more to Alicia and Darla before she went back to her own cabin.

Mganak put his arm around her, and together they watched the boy. She had no idea how much time passed as they waited. Several times the screeching got to be too much for her, and she had to leave for a few minutes to pace anxiously back and forth outside the cabin. Eventually, even Mganak let her persuade him to take a break as well.

Thank goodness there's two of us, she thought when he returned and pulled her onto his lap. How had Darla managed? And how was she going to manage when she was alone with her own child?

CHAPTER EIGHT

A s the night wore on, Davy's voice grew hoarser and his pace finally began to slow as he staggered a little with each step. Wanda prayed that the meltdown was coming to an end.

"I think he is wearing out," Mganak said softly. "If I hold him, can you see if you can get him to take some of the shoko?"

"Are you sure? Darla has made it very clear that he doesn't like to be touched."

"She told me that he responds better to firm pressure." His tail twitched. "I am not sure if it is the right thing to do, but I would like to try."

When she nodded, he went and picked up the boy, immediately wrapping his arms and tail tightly around him but leaving his hands free. Davy gave a startled shriek, but he calmed quickly. Mganak sat down next to her still holding Davy tightly, and she gradually persuaded him to take a drink. After the first taste, he swallowed eagerly. By the time he finished, his body had gone limp. Mganak patted the blanket, and Sagat jumped up next to them. As he began to purr, Mganak laid Davy next to him.

Wanda held her breath, but all Davy did was throw his arm over the rajpar and immediately fall asleep.

"Oh, thank God," she whispered as exhaustion swept over her. Mganak must be just as tired. "Why don't you go get some rest?"

"What about you?"

"I'll be fine. I'll just take a nap tomorrow or something."

"That is not satisfactory. You will be the one to go to bed," he ordered.

His bossiness frayed her already tattered nerves, and she glared at him. Before she could open her mouth and tell him exactly what he could do with his bed, Kareena peeped through the door.

"I heard him quiet," she said softly. "Is he sleeping?"

"Yes, finally. I'm just going to stay here and keep an eye on him," Wanda added, scowling at Mganak.

He scowled back. "You will do nothing of the sort. I will stay with him."

"Why don't you both go to bed?" Kareena offered. "And I will stay with him."

"But you're pregnant. You need your rest."

Kareena shrugged. "I am too big to rest easily. I would be happy to stay with him."

Wanda's exhaustion wrestled with her sense of guilt, but before she could decide what to do, Mganak stood and lifted her into his arms. "Thank you, Kareena."

They were halfway down the corridor before she recovered enough to frown at him. "Kareena needs to rest."

"And so do we, mishka." His annoyance seemed to have vanished as he smiled down at her. "You can see that she rests tomorrow while you take care of the children and I try and keep the ship running."

She wanted to object, but waves of tiredness were still washing over her. Perhaps it was the sensible thing to do.

Mganak carried her up the stairs and straight into the bedroom, laying her down on the big bed. He started to stand back up, but she reached for him, catching his tail in her hand.

"Stay with me," she murmured sleepily, running her fingers along the tantalizing nubbed surface.

She thought she heard him groan, but then he settled in behind her. His arm came around her waist as he pulled her back against the warmth of his body and she stroked his tail again. The last thing she remembered as she drifted off to sleep was feeling him kiss her shoulder.

ONCE AGAIN, WANDA AWOKE TO MGANAK'S TANTALIZING scent, but this time it didn't come from his sheets or his clothes. His body was wrapped around her, surrounding her completely. Her head was pillowed on one of his arms, her legs were entwined with his, his other arm wrapped around her waist and his tail was... His tail was plucking at her aching nipples.

Without conscious thought, she arched into the teasing touch and his grip tightened, sending a delicious shudder of pleasure straight to her clit. She could feel herself dampening, preparing.

"You smell delicious, mishka." Mganak's voice rumbled next to her ear before he licked the delicate shell.

Oh my God. The slightly rough, nubbed surface of his tongue sent another thrill of excitement through her needy body.

"What... What are you doing?" Her voice sounded breathless.

"Exploring."

His hand curved down over her stomach, teasing the small patch of curls at the apex of her thighs. Her legs parted automatically, unable to resist the tantalizing touch. He groaned as he slid a thick digit through her liquid heat.

"You are so wet, mishka. So sweet. I must taste you."

Some distant part of her mind thought about protesting, but before she knew it, he had her on her back, his hands firmly pulling her legs apart as his head disappeared between her thighs. And then he licked her, one long lick from her empty pussy to her throbbing clit. The wide, rough surface awoke every sensitive nerve ending, and she cried out as he brushed her swollen pearl.

He growled and focused there, circling the throbbing flesh and piling sensation upon sensation. His tail whipped back and forth between her breasts, squeezing and plucking at the taut peaks, each firm touch adding to the building fire. She clutched desperately at his broad shoulders and tried to arch into his touch. Her muscles tightened as she perched on the edge of ecstasy, and then a thick digit thrust firmly into her empty pussy and she exploded. Sparks of light danced in front of her eyes at the intensity of the pleasure sweeping over her. She didn't even realize she was calling out his name until her body finally softened and went limp.

He raised his head and smiled at her, a tender smile at odds with the hunger in his dark gaze. She tugged at his shoulders and he rose up over her. She had no thought of denying him—she wanted this, and she wanted him—but when the broad head of his cock pressed against her entrance, impossibly hard and wide, she shivered, and he immediately paused.

"What is it, mishka? Is something wrong?"

"No. Yes. I don't know." Tears suddenly threatened as her brain kicked back on. "I'm just not sure we should be doing this. Nothing has changed since last night."

"Has it not?" he asked gravely and a tear slid down her cheek. Surely he couldn't be hurt by her hesitation. But before she gathered up the courage to ask, he nodded. "Perhaps you are correct. I do not want to cause you concern."

He rolled over on his back and pulled up the sheet but not before she saw the throbbing stiffness of his massive erection. Fudge. How could she be so selfish?

She curled against his side as he stared out at the stars, and she put her hand on his stomach. His firm flesh trembled under her touch.

"What are you doing? Have you changed your mind?"

He sounded so hopeful that another wave of tears threatened, but she shook her head and forced a smile. "No, I still think it's best if we don't go all the way. But..."

Her hand slid down over each impressive ridge of his abdomen until she reached his cock. His breath caught as she circled it with her hand, or at least she tried to. He was far too large for her to enclose in her fist. Still, he didn't complain when she stroked quickly up and down his length. Dark emerald green skin sheathed the hard length, along with more of the nubs that covered the rest of his skin. She could only imagine what that would feel like inside her, and her clit gave an excited little throb.

Mganak's hand stroked her hair as she lowered her face towards him, but when she swiped her tongue across the liquid pearling at his tip, his whole body tensed. He tasted as delicious as he smelled, and she dreamily took another lick.

"What are you doing?" he asked hoarsely. "It is forbidden."

"Forbidden?" As much as she hated to stop, she looked up at him. "You mean like a religious thing?"

"No. We are forbidden to waste our seed because our race is dying." Despite his words, his hand was nudging her mouth back towards his cock.

"You mean you're harvesting it?"

He shook his head, then sighed. "I am a fool. I was told that for so many years—yet what possible difference could it make now?"

"Does that mean you want me to stop? Or not?" She licked him again, and this time she let her teeth scrape gently against the sensitive underside of his cock.

"No! Don't stop."

She hummed with satisfaction, and he groaned again. Thrilled at the way he was responding to her, she gathered her courage and stretched her mouth around the broad head. It was a tight fit, and her jaw immediately began to ache, but he was shaking beneath her, whispering her name over and over. She did her best to relax her mouth and take more of him as she continued to stroke him. His hand tightened in her hair and his body tensed as she managed to take another inch, then two. She hummed again and he exploded with a harsh cry. Jet after jet of hot liquid flooded her mouth, and she did her best to swallow every delicious drop as he shuddered and called out her name.

When the seemingly endless flow finally halted, she swirled her tongue one last time around him and lifted her head. He looked dazed, but his eyes were focused on her. As he pulled her up his body, she realized that he was still hard.

"I don't understand. I know you just came. Why are you still so hard?"

Instead of responding, he kissed her, deeply and thoroughly, his rough tongue adding to the desire already building in her system. When he finally lifted his head, she felt as shaky as he had looked.

"You are a wonder, mishka," he said. "I had no idea that a female's mouth could be so fulfilling."

"You mean you never..."

"Never. We were indoctrinated with the idea that it was forbidden."

"Oh." She frowned as she thought about what he'd said. No wonder he had seemed so overwhelmed. She had thought it was because of her, but perhaps it was just a new experience. "Well, now you know," she said briskly and tried to sit up.

He stopped her by the simple expedient of rolling her over beneath him. "I do not think you understand. The act has been offered to me before, but I was never tempted. I had no desire to reconsider why it was forbidden. But you, mishka—I could never resist you."

"But you're still hard." The evidence was pressing tantalizingly against her needy body.

"In order to find a full release, a Cire male must knot inside his mate's body."

"Knot?"

"The base of my cock will swell and lock us together."

She gulped, even as her pussy clenched eagerly at the notion.

"You mean once you find a mate?" Why did that thought fill her with despair?

"I already... Yes, of course." He swung them up into a sitting position. "The lights will be up soon. We should see how everyone is this morning."

"Of course." She couldn't keep the desolate tone out of her voice, and he put his arm and tail around her and hugged her close.

"There is nowhere else that I want to be and no one else that I would rather be with. We may not have forever, but at least we have now."

"Alicia said something like that yesterday."

"I think she has great wisdom."

"I suspect you're right. So we will meet the day together."

"Together," he agreed.

For now. The unspoken words echoed in her head, but she took his hand and went to face the day.

CHAPTER NINE

The hardest thing Mganak had ever done was to let Wanda leave his bed. He wanted to bury himself in her willing body, to prove to her that she was his mate. He had suspected it from the first moment his tail had reached for her in the crowded lifeboat, when he had breathed in her delicious scent. Now he knew it without a shadow of a doubt, but how could he ask her to give up her child's future for him?

He could understand why she would want to bring up the child on her home planet. If he had a child, he would want to bring it up on Ciresia—well, perhaps not. The planet was little more than a mausoleum as the survivors tried desperately to save their dying race. But he still understood the sentiment and he could not hold her back.

Trying his best to restrain himself, he was delighted when she and the children decided to spend the morning with him. Darla was showing Wanda how she cleaned the filters when Davy suddenly made a distressed sound. Mganak looked over to find the young male beginning to rock back and forth, and mutter under his breath. Normally, Sagat was very responsive to any indication that the boy was feeling overwhelmed, but for once, he did not rush to Davy's side. Instead, he prowled in a circle around the room, shaking his own head.

"Is something wrong?" Wanda asked as Darla went to her brother's side.

"I do not know, but something is obviously bothering both of them."

Sagat paced to the door of the workshop, then paused, shaking his head again.

"I am going to take a look in the cargo hold. Wait here."

As soon as he opened the door, he heard it. A low beeping sound came from the abandoned lifeboat. The emergency beacon that should have been active while the women and children were on board had suddenly started up. But why now? Was there some type of fault in the wiring?

Regardless of the cause, there was no need for the signal, and he went to terminate it. The usual controls did not seem to have any effect and it took him more time than he had expected before he tracked down the source of the signal and turned it off. In the meantime, he could hear Sagat whining as Davy's distress increased.

When he finally managed to deactivate the signal, Sagat immediately settled, going to Davy and pressing against him but the boy took longer to calm. When he finally settled, Darla took him upstairs, leaving Mganak alone with Wanda.

"What's wrong?" she asked. "You look worried."

"I do not know if I should be concerned or not. The controls on board the vessel appear to be nothing more than decoys. The real control was located outside the ship."

"I don't understand. Doesn't that mean that no one would be able to operate it from inside?"

"Exactly," he said grimly. "Which makes me wonder who

was intended to control it and if they are the ones who triggered it now."

Her eyes widened. "You mean the Vedeckians?"

He hated to see the distress on her face but he wasn't going to lie to her. "It seems like the most obvious possibility."

"So we are valuable. They simply didn't turn on the beacon before because they didn't want anyone else picking up their cargo. And now they're looking for us?"

His protective instincts raged at terrified look on her face and he swept her up in his arms, heading for the stairs at a rapid pace. He wasn't going to waste time waiting for the lift.

"Do you think you turned it off in time?" she whispered.

He prayed to Granthar that he had, but he wasn't about to take any chances. "I do not know. It would depend on how close they were when they initiated the signal. In the meantime, I am getting us out of here."

"What do you mean?"

"If they did pick up the signal for any length of time, it would not be difficult to project our destination. We are going to have to take another route."

Soon as they reached the landing, he placed her on her feet. "Tell everyone to return to their beds and fasten the harnesses. I might have to make some fast maneuvers and I do not want anyone getting hurt."

Despite the urgency beating at him, he paused long enough to press a quick kiss to her lips. "Hurry, mishka. As soon as I reset our course, I will come back to you."

She bit her lip but nodded. He raced to the bridge and immediately shifted to an alternate vector, pulling up a star chart as he did. This was a relatively uninhabited sector of the galaxy with few places to hide. Except...

He rubbed his face, trying to decide if he should take the

chance when Wanda called to him from the bottom of the stairs.

"Everyone is in their beds. Sagat is with the children," she said when he went to get her.

"Are they all right?"

"Yes, but they're scared. I'm scared."

"I know, mishka, but I will do everything I can to keep you safe." He hesitated on the landing. "Do you want to join me on the bridge?"

"Yes please. I would rather know what's going on."

He lifted her into the other chair and fastened the harness. She looks so small and helpless in the big pilot seat. The Vedeckians were not going to get their hands on her—on any of them—he vowed.

Just as he resumed his own seat, the proximity alarm pinged. *Fuck.* It looked as if he didn't have a choice now.

"I am going to have to try and hide the ship," he told Wanda. "But first, I am going to leave a distraction."

He altered course a few times, hopefully making it appear that he was uncertain as to his destination. The ship skittered with each rapid move, but each time he changed direction, he dropped a floating mine. He had picked them up a few years ago, but he'd been unwilling to sell them, concerned about the destruction they might cause if they fell into the wrong hands. Right now, he was all for destruction.

The comm beeped. The Vedeckian ship was hailing him.

Wanda's hands were clenched tightly on the arms of her chair, but she hadn't protested as the ship jumped from position to position. As the comm beeped again, she shot him a worried look.

"What's that?"

"The Vedeckian ship is trying to contact us."

"Are you going to talk to them?"

He shook his head. "There is no point. They will demand that I give you up, and I am not going to do that. And there is no reason why I should provide them with any information about me or about this ship. I am recording any incoming message so we can listen to it later."

The light on the recorder blinked, but he ignored it. The comm went silent, but he didn't make the mistake of relaxing. A minute ticked by, another, and then something hit the rear of the ship, the impact throwing them to one side.

"What was that? Did they damage us?"

"No, but they tried." With a heavy sigh, he clicked the switch that would activate the mines. He had hoped he wouldn't have to use them, but if they were firing on the ship, there was no other choice. "I have activated our defenses, but we are still close. If they fire, we are likely to get tossed around—"

The second explosion occurred before he finished speaking. This time, the whole bridge tilted to the left. *Fuck.* He had hoped they would be further away before the Vedeckian ship triggered any of the mines.

"Hang on," he said grimly, then abandoned all evasive maneuvers and headed straight for the asteroid belt.

It was a calculated risk. He knew the area, knew it all too well, but that didn't mean he was oblivious to the danger it represented. A glancing blow against one of the larger asteroids, or even a bombardment from the small ones, could cause serious damage to his ship.

But the Vedeckian ship was much larger and less maneuverable than his. It would be even more at risk if they tried to follow him into the belt.

A third explosion followed, and this time an alarm sounded as all of the lights switched off. He heard Wanda gasp in the darkness before the emergency lights came on. In the dim red glow, he could see her face was pale and frightened. He silenced the alarm, worried about how Davy would react to the noise, but he left the emergency lighting alone as he scanned his monitors.

He swore again. "That one hit us, I am afraid."

"What about the others?"

"They are fine. It was a glancing blow to the rear engine compartment. I am not going to try and restore internal power yet. I am going to take us in there and then shut everything down."

Wanda's eyes widened even further as she took in the chaos of the asteroid belt, but she didn't protest. His brave little mishka.

Yet another explosion came from behind them, but it was far enough away to do little more than send a shudder through the ship. Good. They were increasing the distance from the Vedeckian ship. No doubt the other captain thought he had them trapped.

An asteroid easily as large as his ship reared in front of them, and he yanked the controls to the right. More obstacles followed but he darted around them, gaining confidence as he remembered the necessary skills.

The ship jerked and spun with each maneuver, but once again, Wanda didn't protest. As they neared the center of the belt, another one of the larger asteroids appeared in front of them. This time he didn't maneuver around it but came to a halt as close to the surface as he could manage, then immediately cut the engine. He killed all of the systems except for the minimum needed to maintain life support and one external monitor.

They waited in tense silence, but there were no additional explosions and the Vedeckian ship made no attempt to enter the asteroid belt. At last, he sighed and sat back.

"Is everything all right? Are we safe now?" Wanda's voice was hoarse with strain and, after another check of the monitor, he released her from her chair and pulled her into his lap. His tail curved around her waist and he wasn't sure if it was to reassure her or for his own benefit. He buried his nose in her hair and breathed in her sweet scent.

"Is everyone else okay?" she asked anxiously.

He pointed to another panel. "Their vital signs are good. As soon as I verify the status of the ship, we can go and check on them."

It was a little awkward running diagnostics with her in his arms, but he wasn't ready to let her go yet. Life support was in full working order. Communications were undamaged, and he didn't pick up any indication of damage to the hull. He was about to breathe a sigh of relief when the diagnostics completed on the engine compartment. *Fuck.*

Wanda must have felt him tense because she bit her lip as she looked up at him. "What's wrong?"

"It looks as if the hyperdrive is damaged."

"What does that mean? Are we stuck here?"

"No, but it drastically reduces our speed. It would take weeks to get to Ayuul."

She looked oddly thoughtful but she didn't comment. He checked again, hoping that he was wrong, then sighed.

"I am afraid I am going to have to get this repaired."

"You can't repair it yourself?"

"Unfortunately not." He could almost have laughed at the irony. The more he tried to escape his past, the more it reared its ugly head. "There is a repair shop within a reasonable distance, even at reduced speed. I will have to take it there."

"Is that a problem?" She reached up and pressed her soft hand to his cheek. "You look worried. Will we be in danger?"

"I would never permit anyone to harm you" he assured her

truthfully. "At one time, I would have trusted Rafalo with my life." *Could he still?* He only wished he knew for sure.

"Is he someone you know?"

"Unfortunately. He was the captain of the ship I stowed away on when I left Ciresia."

Her mouth opened, but before she could ask any questions he did not want to answer, he stood, carrying her with him. "Let us go check on the others."

CHAPTER TEN

W anda studied Mganak's face as he carried her silently down the stairs. He was frowning into the distance, his body even tenser than it had been during the battle with the Vedeckian ship. He had said this Captain Rafalo wasn't a threat. Why did he look so worried?

When he had mentioned the male before, he had seemed equally reluctant to discuss him yet he had said that he was the one who had taught him. What had happened between the two of them?

They reached the bottom of the stairs, but he didn't put her down. If anything, he gathered her more closely against him, his tail clinging to her.

"If you don't want to repair the ship at this place, we don't have to go there," she said softly, then shrugged. "So it takes a little longer to get to Ayuul. It's fine."

And she truly didn't mind, she realized. She was happy here on the ship with Mganak. Earth seemed very far away.

For the first time, he seemed to relax as he looked solemnly down at her. "I promised you that I would help you find your way home. And it is not just a question of the increased length of time. We would need to take on additional supplies, and Rafalo's station is the closest place to acquire those."

He bent his head and kissed her. Perhaps he had intended it as nothing more than a reassurance, but as always, the heat flared between them. But it was more than just desire, there was a desperate urgency in his kiss that touched her heart. If not for the need to check on the others, she would have dragged him back up to their room.

He seemed to come to his senses at the same time she did and lifted his head, his face soft and smiling despite the hard cock throbbing against her buttocks.

"You make me forget myself, mishka."

"Ditto." She laughed at his puzzled look. "It means you have the same effect on me. Now put me down and let's go reassure everyone."

In the children's cabin, Darla greeted them anxiously. Davy was asleep, pressed up against Sagat.

"Is everything all right?" the girl asked. "Why are the lights red?"

"We are operating under minimal power so that we cannot be detected," Mganak said reassuringly.

Wanda wasn't sure that she would have provided the girl with that much information, but Darla nodded as if she understood.

Alicia frowned when they gave her the all clear and explained the delay, but somewhat to Wanda's surprise, she didn't protest. She had been afraid the older woman would react more negatively to the knowledge that it would take longer to return home. Instead, Alicia shrugged an elegant shoulder.

"I don't suppose it makes much difference at this point. We

have been gone so long that any explanation is going to be difficult."

They reached the medical lab and found Kareena crouched in the corner.

"Why didn't you use the harness?" Wanda scolded as she rushed to the other female's side. "Are you hurt?"

"I'm not hurt. I was strapped in until I felt the ship come to a halt. Are they still out there? Is he coming for me?"

"We're safe," Wanda said quickly. "We're hiding in an asteroid belt. No one followed us in here. Why did you get down?"

"I was going to try and hide." A red tear rolled down Kareena's cheek. "But then..."

Her whole body tensed, and Wanda watched in horror as her stomach rippled. "Oh my God. You're in labor."

Kareena breathed through the contraction then nodded. Wanda heard Alicia gasp quietly, then turn to Darla and urge her out of the room.

"Don't worry," Wanda said as calmly as possible. "I'm sure everything is going to be fine. Let's start by getting you off the floor. Mganak, can you put her back on the bed?"

Kareena shuddered but she didn't protest as Mganak placed her gently on the bed. He fiddled with the controls for a minute, then managed to raise the back half so that Kareena was in a sitting position. The other female gave him a shaky smile as Wanda tried desperately to remember everything she had read recently about giving birth. And was a human birth the same as a Vedeckian birth?

Tugging Mganak to one side, she whispered frantically. "You said this was a medical lab. Is there anything here that can help us?"

"I also said I never finish setting it up. But let me see what I can do."

He started searching through the bank of cabinets while Wanda covered Kareena with a blanket, then held her hand. She didn't have a watch but the next contraction occurred far too quickly for her liking. *Fudge.* What was she going to do?

"Is there anything you can tell me about giving birth amongst your people?"

More red tinged tears dripped down Kareena's cheeks as she shook her head. "Each household has an older female to assist with the birth. Kane was taking me to the one in his household before I made him angry and he put me in with you."

Double fudge.

"Giving birth is a perfectly natural act. I'm sure everything is going to be fine." Wanda was amazed at how calm she sounded.

Mganak made a triumphant noise and a moment later a screen descended from the ceiling. An illuminated bar swept out from the bottom of it, scanning the length of Kareena's body. Information flashed up on the screen, but to Wanda, it was nothing more than a blur of colored lights and strange symbols.

"Can you read that?" she asked Mganak.

"Some of the terminology is unfamiliar to me but I understand the basics. The child does not seem to be in distress."

"What about the mother?" she hissed, hoping that Kareena couldn't hear her.

"Everything seems to be satisfactory." He hesitated. "Do you want me to leave? Many races only allow females during a birth."

"Oh no you don't. You're the only one who can read that thing. And humans insist on the male being present," she added firmly. Not that she would have one there for her child's birth, she thought with a pang, but this wasn't about her.

Returning to Kareena's side, she held her hand and encouraged her to breathe through the next contraction. The time between the last one and this one seemed even shorter, and she had a feeling that time was running out.

Kareena was wearing a simple black shift cut from another of Mganak shirts. "Do you want to take your dress off?" she asked quietly, and the other female nodded gratefully.

Mganak looked as if he wanted to run for the door again, but she gestured him back behind the bed as she assisted Kareena in removing the dress. Oddly enough, despite the other female's obvious trepidation about Mganak, she didn't seem concerned about her nudity. Nonetheless, Wanda draped the blanket back over her just as another contraction hit.

The monitor beeped. "What does it say?"

Mganak reluctantly emerged from behind the bed so that he could read the screen. "It is time. It says you should help her with her breathing and cleanse the birthing site."

"Well, I can't do both." She sighed. "Kareena, would it be all right if Mganak helped you with your breathing?"

"It is not allowed," Kareena whispered, but then her hand tightened on Wanda's as another contraction swept through her. "But if it will help my baby, then I will permit it."

Despite his obvious reluctance, Mganak's hands were gentle as he took Wanda's place at Kareena's side. A tray with additional equipment had emerged from one of the cabinets. At least some of it was familiar to Wanda, and with Mganak interpreting the monitor and what she could remember from her own reading, she prepared for the birth.

Kareena never complained, and after what seemed like an eternity, a small white infant slid into Wanda's waiting hands. When the baby didn't cry out, she was terrified that something had gone wrong, but then she looked down and saw the child's eyes were wide open. Grateful tears streamed down her cheeks as she cleansed the baby and handed her to Kareena. Kareena was crying too, still silently, as she gathered her child to her breast.

Wanda looked up and saw Mganak watching her rather than the new mother. There was a wistfulness on his face as he looked at her and she wondered if he was thinking the same thing. How much she would love to have him there when it was her turn to give birth. All of her determination to go through it alone suddenly seemed hollow.

Tearing her eyes away, she found the nursing drink the monitor had recommended and offered it to Kareena. The other female barely noticed, unable to tear her eyes away from her daughter's face.

"She's so beautiful," she whispered. "I have to find a way to protect her."

"We'll do everything we can to help you," Wanda promised. "Do you need anything else?"

"I... I would like to be alone with my daughter if that's all right. It's not that I'm ungrateful..."

"It's all right. I understand. Just call out if you need anything." She gave Mganak an uncertain look. "Is there some kind of intercom?"

He nodded and placed a small panel next to Kareena. "Use this if you require assistance." He hesitated, then gave a formal bow. "May Granthar bless you and your child."

Kareena looked shocked, then inclined her head with equal formality. "Thank you, Mganak of Cire."

Mganak nodded once, then escorted Wanda out of the room. As soon at the door closed behind them, her knees threatened to collapse.

"We did it! I was so scared."

"You did very well, my mishka." Mganak put a large warm

hand over her stomach. "I did not truly understand what is involved in giving birth. I wish—"

Whatever he intended to say was cut off as Darla peeked anxiously down the corridor. "Is everything okay?"

"Yes, it's fine. Kareena has a brand-new daughter."

"Yay! Another girl."

"We will talk later," Mganak said softly, before they went to meet the girl. "You have no use for male children?" he teased.

"Girls are better," Darla said firmly, then grinned up at him. "But some of you are okay."

"Thank you. I am relieved that you can tolerate our companionship."

Darla grinned again and patted his arm. "Come see what we did."

"I can see that you did more damage to my wardrobe," he said ruefully as Darla showed them a small pile of what had to be diapers while Alicia held up a small gown.

"Do you mind?"

"Not at all. It was very thoughtful of you."

"I help," Davy said proudly as he stacked the diapers in the neat line.

"I can see that. Good job, son."

Davy gave a satisfied nod, but Wanda heard Darla catch her breath. Did Mganak realize what he had said?

Alicia stepped into the silence, holding up a large plastic container from the kitchen, now padded and lined with fabric. "We made this as well. For the baby to sleep in."

There was an oddly hesitant note in the other woman's voice. Wanda realized that for once her clothes were rumpled and her hair was out of place. But she looked happy.

"I think that's a wonderful idea. Kareena wanted a little time alone with the baby, but I'm sure she'll be thrilled. And hungry. Maybe I could try making that soup you made?"

"No." The other four spoke simultaneously, and Wanda blushed.

"You have many fine qualities, mishka, but cooking is not one of your skills. I will prepare the shol and then go set our course."

"Are you gonna put the lights back on?" Darla asked.

"Eventually. But I would like to be further away from here before I do so." He turned back to Wanda. "Now you will sit down and rest."

She wanted to argue with him, but her legs still felt weak and exhaustion swept over her. After murmuring a token protest, she curled up in one of his oversized chairs. Davy followed Mganak into the kitchen, and Alicia began showing Darla how to make another little gown for the baby. As she closed her eyes and drifted off to sleep, the contented sounds of her odd little family filled her with happiness.

CHAPTER ELEVEN

"We are approaching the station now," Mganak said, and Wanda peered eagerly through the viewport.

She had joined him on the bridge, partially because she wanted to see their destination and partially because she could tell that he was worried about the upcoming visit. They had spent the last five days slowly working their way through the asteroid belt and there was an odd sense that time had been suspended. Everything felt as if it was on hold, even as they went about their daily business. Mganak continued to work on minor updates and repairs, with Darla's enthusiastic assistance, and both Wanda and Davy frequently joined them. She loved watching him interact with the children, but then he would look over at her and the heat would flare between them.

The teaching program that Mganak located was very effective, and both she and Darla made a tremendous amount of progress in reading Galactic Standard. Kareena wandered around in a daze of happiness, completely preoccupied with her new daughter, Kanda. Alicia helped as much as she could, both with the baby and the children.

And every night, she and Mganak explored each other. There wasn't an inch of her body that he hadn't kissed and caressed, and they spent each night wrapped in each other's arms. But they hadn't fully consummated their attraction. Wanda ached for him, and his desire for her was equally obvious, but she just couldn't bring herself to take that final step. She wasn't going to stay with him. She couldn't stay with him. And... he hadn't asked her to stay.

"Is that where we're going?" Wanda asked as a giant moon grew ever larger in the viewport. "That moon?"

"That is not a moon. It is a space station. It was artificially constructed and put into orbit around Tyssia many generations ago."

"Tyssia?"

Before Mganak had a chance to answer, a planet started to emerge on the left side of the viewport. A huge lavender ball, pink clouds swirled lazily over the surface. "Wow. It's beautiful!"

"Yes, it is. Unfortunately, it is also uninhabitable."

"Why is that?"

"The atmosphere is not suitable for lifeforms that rely on oxygen."

"What a shame." She reluctantly tore her eyes away from the beautiful planet and focused on the upcoming space station instead. It definitely suffered by comparison. As they grew closer, she could see that much of the outer surface looked dented and dirty. Perhaps once it had been a pristine white, but now it looked more as if someone had sent a ping-pong ball into a muddy gutter.

"Are you sure it's safe?"

He nodded, but his mouth straightened into a grim line. "Despite his other faults—his many other faults—Rafalo always took good care of his equipment."

"And this is his place?"

"Not just his, although he is the... leader. But there are, of course, all the other businesses you might expect to find on a space station."

"Do you think they have a clothing store?"

"You are tired of wearing my clothing, mishka?" His face softened as he smiled at her. "I would have no objection if you wished to abandon clothing altogether."

"On the ship with three children and two other women?" she asked dryly.

"Perhaps you have a point. As for the prospect of clothing..." He looked grim again. "I expect anything you find will be more suitable for a pleasure companion."

She curved her hand over her stomach. "In other words, it's unlikely to fit me—not that I think I'm the pleasure companion type. But really I wasn't asking for myself. I thought it would be nice to be able to buy or make some clothes for Kanda. It just doesn't seem right to have a baby dressed in black."

His eyes had heated and he didn't seem to be listening to her. "Mganak?"

"Forgive me, mishka. I was envisioning you dressed as a pleasure companion." The warmth in his eyes sent a pleasurable shiver down her spine. "But even if there is no appropriate clothing, perhaps we could purchase fabric for the child."

"That would be nice. And maybe something for Davy and Darla as well." Guilt washed over her. "I'm sorry. I'm being very free with your money."

"I have already told you that everything I have is yours."

A lump appeared in her throat, but before she could decide how to respond, he had already continued. "But if you do not wish to be beholden to me, it occurs to me that you could sell the lifeboat."

"But that's not mine."

"I believe you could make a valid argument that it was given into your possession. It would be small recompense for the damage the Vedeckians have caused to your life—to all of your lives."

"I hadn't really thought about it like that. I'll talk to Kareena and see what she thinks."

"As you—"

Before he could finish, the comm pinged a demand for identification. His face immediately turned grim again.

"This is Captain Mganak Sar'Taren of *The Wanderer*. I wish to dock and undergo repairs."

"Oh, you do, do you?" A deep voice growled. "And what under Hebra's stars make you think I should allow that?"

Mganak's tail lashed anxiously, and Wanda automatically reached for it. At her touch, it calmed and curled around her hand.

"I have females and children on board," Mganak said evenly. "If you are as concerned about their welfare as you wish me to believe, you will permit me to land."

"Slaves?" The voice mocked. "How far the self-righteous have fallen."

Mganak's tail tightened so strongly around her hand that her fingers ached, but she didn't protest. Whatever was happening between these two, she was on his side.

"They are not slaves. I... rescued them."

A roar of laughter came through the comm. "Oh, Mganak. Isn't it ironic? Surely you appreciate the situation."

Mganak didn't respond and after a brief silence, the speaker sighed. "Very well. Use Dock 19. I wouldn't want my reputation sullied by associating with a possible slave owner."

Mganak growled as he slammed his hand down to disconnect the communication.

"Was that Rafalo?" she asked softly.

"I am afraid so."

"What happened between the two of you?"

"I apparently misjudged him." His tail tightened around her hand again. "At the time, I had no doubt, but I found out later—not from him—that I was wrong. He knew that I had misunderstood, and he chose not to enlighten me because he thought I should trust him."

"It's not your fault that he didn't explain."

"No, that is what I told myself. But we had been close for a long time and perhaps I should have understood that there was more to the situation than met the eye."

She gave his tail a soothing pat. "We've all been wrong before."

"It is not a situation I enjoy," he muttered as he returned his attention to the controls.

No, she couldn't imagine that her big honorable warrior did enjoy discovering that he had been wrong. She watched silently as he piloted the ship around the space station and towards an opening that seemed far too small.

"Isn't the ship too big?" She couldn't help asking as the ship grew closer to the tiny entrance.

"I will make it fit." Mganak's solemnity vanished for a moment as his tail reached over to curl around her breast. "I am very good at making large objects fit into small spaces."

She laughed and squeezed his tail before pushing it away, even though the teasing words and the even more teasing touch had started her thoughts in an entirely different direction.

True to his word, Mganak steered easily through the open doors, then sat back and sighed. "It will not take long to restore oxygen to the dock. And for Rafalo to come poking his nose around."

"Are you going to talk to him?"

"I suspect that I will not have a choice."

"Is it safe for us to get off the ship?" She peered out of the viewport at the dock surrounding them. Various pieces of equipment were stacked rather haphazardly around the sides of the space and like the outer surface of the space station, it looked dirty and rather decrepit, but at least it would be a change from the ship.

"Only if I accompany you." Mganak rubbed his face. "I will go see if Rafalo has shown his face and arrange to get the repairs started. If everything looks safe, then perhaps I could accompany you and Alicia to the market area."

He stood, then bent down and ran a finger along the low edge of her neckline. "I do not suppose you have anything more concealing?"

She felt herself flush, and he used his finger to follow the wave of pink. Her breasts seemed to increase in size every day, and even though the dress had fit perfectly when Alicia made it, it now felt like they were about to spill out of her gown. Her stomach too was growing, clearly visible beneath the soft material.

"I'm pretty sure you're familiar with everything in my wardrobe," she said tartly, trying to cover her embarrassment. "Are you ashamed of me?"

He looked genuinely shocked. "I could never be ashamed of you, mishka. I simply do not wish to have to fight off the other males you will attract."

"Don't be ridiculous." The heat in her cheeks increased. "I doubt anyone is interested in a rather ordinary pregnant human."

"You are very far from ordinary." This time his hand slipped under the neckline and curved around one of her breasts. His other hand went to her stomach. "You are lush and beautiful, glowing with life. No male could resist you."

He sounded so uncertain that she lifted a hand to his cheek. "You know that I don't want any other male, don't you?"

"I am glad," he said simply. "You are my ma... mishka."

Why did she think he had intended to say something else? Her pulse thudded rapidly in her veins but before she could gather up the courage to ask him, Darla's excited voice reached them as the girl raced up the stairs.

"This place is so cool. Is that red machine one of the pulse generators you were telling me about?"

"It is," Mganak said evenly. "But how did you know? You were supposed to remain in your bunk until I came to release you."

"Oops." Darla gave him an unrepentant grin. "The ship came to a halt and I didn't hear any shooting, so I peeked out the window. I figured it would be all right. Can I go out and look at all the equipment?"

"No." When her face fell, Mganak relented. "Not yet, anyway. Once I am sure of the situation, you can take a look around. Where is Davy?"

"Playing with his container of screws." Darla sighed. "He doesn't even care that we're on a space station."

"As long as he's happy, that's all that matters," Wanda said gently.

"I know. But it's so exciting!" The girl gave Mganak a pleading look. "Can you go see if it's safe now? Please?"

"I am on my way." Mganak gathered Wanda up in his arms. "I suppose you are going to want to see more as well."

"You know I am." She leaned in and pressed a teasing kiss to his neck, reveling in the intriguing texture that met her mouth. "I always want to see more."

"Ooh." Darla made a face as she clattered along next to them. "Stop all the mushy stuff."

"But I enjoy this so-called mushy stuff," Mganak said

solemnly.

"Yeah, yeah. How would you feel if I started getting mushy with someone?"

Mganak growled. "That will never happen."

Wanda's breath caught, and she hid her face in Mganak's neck, even as the other two continued to banter. It was so easy to forget that he wouldn't be there when Darla grew up, when she started to date. Even if Wanda were able to adopt Davy and Darla as she so desperately wished, Darla would never have a father like Mganak. And what if she couldn't adopt them? What if her disappearance changed things enough that she wouldn't be considered a good candidate? Her heart filled with dread.

All of the thoughts, all of the concerns that she had pushed aside for the last week came roaring back. They had formed a family—not just her and the children but all of them—and Mganak was an essential part of it. She didn't want to take the children away from him. She didn't want to leave him.

The baby kicked as if in agreement, and Wanda felt Mganak's arms tighten at the small movement. But was it best for her child if she stayed? Could she bring her up here, on a spaceship?

Mganak set her down as they reached the hold. He gave her a concerned look, as if he sensed her worries, and his tail curved comfortingly around her wrist. "Is something wrong, mishka? I do believe that you will be safe here. I will not let anything happen to you."

She managed a shaky smile. "I know you won't."

Alicia came down the stairs to join them. "What's the plan? Kareena is worried about anyone knowing she's here. She says everyone hates Vedeckians so she's staying in the lounge with Kanda and keeping an eye on Davy. Sagat is keeping watch over all of them."

"I am going to arrange for the repairs," Mganak said, his voice confident. "All of you will remain here while I make the arrangements."

Despite his calmness, Wanda's heart skipped a beat when he retrieved a weapon from a locked cabinet and put the holster around his waist.

"Is that necessary?" she whispered.

"I do not expect so, but I would rather have it and not need it than the reverse." He hesitated, then reached into the cabinet and withdrew a second weapon. "Here. Again, I do not expect that it will be necessary, but I want you to have it, just in case."

"What about me?" Alicia asked.

Mganak looked almost as surprised as Wanda felt at Alicia's request. The older woman simply raised an eyebrow. "I assure you that I am a competent shot."

"Very well." He handed Alicia a third weapon.

"Me too," Darla demanded.

"No!" The three adults spoke simultaneously, and she glared at them.

"I should be able to defend myself."

"Have you ever used a weapon?" Mganak asked.

"Well, no," she admitted. "But you know I'm a fast learner."

"Then I will teach you, but this is not the time and place for that lesson." Mganak put a big hand on the girl's thin shoulder. "It damages the soul to perform an act of violence against another, even if it is necessary. Let us spare you that."

Darla gave a reluctant nod, and Mganak turned back to Wanda. "Keep the door locked. You can watch what's happening on the monitor."

A thousand protests threatened to escape, but in the end, she simply nodded. He dropped a brief kiss on her lips and disappeared through the door panel.

CHAPTER TWELVE

W anda watched anxiously through the monitor as Mganak descended the landing ramp. Both the picture and the sound in the monitor were crystal clear, and she could hear the quiet clang of his boots hitting the ramp. But the angle of the camera didn't cover the entire space, and when he froze, his hand going to the holstered weapon, she couldn't see who he was looking at. What if there was a group of people out there and he was outnumbered?

Her fingers clenched, fighting the urge to unlock the door and join him. Alicia put a cool hand over hers.

"Just wait," the older woman said quietly. "He doesn't look alarmed."

"Maybe he's just too brave for his own good," she muttered, but Alicia's calm composure helped soothe her nerves. Besides, the other woman was right. Mganak looked alert but not concerned.

Then the figure he had apparently seen shuffled into sight and her nerves settled even further. Stooped and obviously elderly, with wrinkled orange scales, the new alien looked far from threatening. A grease stained overall covered a short, stocky body.

"So you decided to come back, did you?"

Despite the hoarse voice, Wanda realized with a start that the newcomer was female.

"I am not back. I sustained damage to my hyperdrive."

Rheumy old eyes peered at Mganak from beneath a ridged brow. "And how did that happen?"

"A hit from a Vedeckian ship."

The old female shook her head. "You always did like to live dangerously, boy."

"I was never aware that I had a choice, Emtal. You know as well as I do that Rafalo attracts trouble."

Emtal shrugged. "You never complained."

"I did not know any better." He held up his hand when the female appeared ready to continue the argument. "Can you just take a look at the ship, please?"

Emtal grunted, but she nodded and the two of them disappeared out of view of the monitor. Wanda waited anxiously while Darla danced around impatiently, staring at the monitor.

"I should be out there. I want to know what they're going to do."

"I'm sure Mganak will tell you all about it," Alicia said. "And the two of you can discuss it in endless detail."

Wanda gave her a sympathetic grin. As much as she enjoyed seeing Mganak and Darla bond over their mutual interest in mechanics, she agreed with Alicia that their discussions could get a little tedious.

After what seemed like an eternity but was probably only a few minutes, Mganak and Emtal reappeared. The old woman was rubbing her hands together gleefully and Mganak looked resigned but not worried.

"Yep, definitely going to be expensive," Emtal cackled.

"Your charges are outrageous."

"I wouldn't charge an old friend as much, but since you're just passing through..." Emtal shrugged, then turned toward the unseen entrance to the dock. "Come here, boy."

A second alien appeared. A head taller than the old female, he still looked almost childlike next to Mganak's big body. He was a child, Wanda decided as she studied him, or at least a teenager. A slender young male with blue patterned skin and long white hair, he rather resembled an elf due to his delicate features and pointed ears.

"Who's that?" Darla sighed.

Wanda looked down to find the girl staring at the newcomer with unabashed admiration. Fudge. The last thing they needed was for the girl to get a crush on this boy.

"He's probably just here to run some errands," she said dismissively, but then her heart sank when Emtal began issuing a series of commands that made it quite clear that the boy was a junior mechanic.

Darla's eyes opened even wider, and she gave another dreamy sigh. "Did you hear that? She's gonna let him take the crystals out of the drive compartment."

"Perhaps he will let you watch," Alicia suggested, smiling when Wanda glared at her.

"Do you think so? I'm gonna go get my tablet so I can take notes." Darla raced off.

"Now why did you say that?" Wanda demanded of Alicia as soon as the girl was out of earshot.

"What did you intend to do? Refuse to let her see him?" The other woman raised one of her delicately arched eyebrows. "You know that would only have made him more attractive in her eyes."

"She's just a little girl."

"I was her age the first time I saw Thomas. I never looked at anyone else after that."

"But she's only twelve."

"I'm not suggesting that they should rush off and get married. Right now, I suspect she is as interested in him for his mechanical skills as she is for anything else. As my mother used to say, don't borrow trouble."

Wanda sighed. "Easy for you to say."

"Is that really what you think?" Alicia's tone was as cool and composed as ever, but Wanda caught the flash of hurt in her eyes.

"No, I don't. I'm sorry. I know you care just as much about the children as I do." It was quite true. Even though Alicia had a harder time expressing her feelings, Wanda knew she loved the children.

"I do," Alicia said softly, then laughed. "And besides, if you think for one second that Mganak would ever let anything happen to her... As I suspect that boy is about to find out."

All three were now approaching the landing ramp. Mganak stalked up it and threw open the door. Wanda studied his face anxiously, but he looked annoyed rather than concerned as he ushered the other two on board.

"Wanda, this is Emtal. Despite her bedraggled appearance, she's the best mechanic in the sector."

"Or any sector. And no point in getting fancy before you tear an engine apart." Emtal's eyes might have been clouded by age, but they appeared disconcertingly sharp as she scanned Wanda's face. "Huh. Well, that explains a lot."

"Explains what?" Mganak demanded.

Instead of responding, the old female cackled and turned to Alicia. "Are you part of the harem?"

"I most certainly am not." Alicia raised an eyebrow and nodded at the young male. "Is he part of yours?"

The boy looked appalled even as Emtal roared with laughter. "Oh, I like you, girl. I don't suppose you're a mechanic?"

"Not in the least. I hire people to do that for me," Alicia said coldly, obviously still offended by the previous question.

Wanda winced, but Emtal didn't seem bothered.

"Probably for the best. It's a messy business, and I can't say much for the company. Eh, boy?" She nudged the young male in his ribs so hard that he winced, but he gave her an affectionate smile.

"I've never had any reason to complain."

Emtal shook her head. "If I hadn't seen you work on an engine, I'd be sure you were headed for the diplomatic corps. Now then, let's take a look at the engine compartment."

"It's over here. I... I can take you." Darla came racing up, but her rush of words came to a rapid halt as she stared at the young man.

Fudge. He returned her stare just as avidly until Emtal reached over and cuffed the back of his head.

"What's wrong with you, boy? Never seen a girl before?"

He ignored her, still staring at Darla. "I am Tanik. I am honored to make your acquaintance."

"I'm Darla." The girl gave him a shy smile.

Wanda saw the exact moment when Mganak realized what was happening. He let out an outraged growl and stepped between the two.

"You should return to your brother," he ordered Darla.

"You said I could watch."

"The repairs, not the mechanic."

Darla's pale cheeks flushed as she scowled at him, and Wanda remembered Alicia's earlier words. "She's just going to watch," she said quickly. "Does this mean it's all right for Alicia and me to go out in the station?"

As she hoped, the question distracted him. He stopped

HONEY PHILLIPS & BEX MCLYNN

glaring at Tanik long enough to give her a worried frown. "I am not sure."

"Oh, for heaven's sake." Emtal gave an exasperated huff. "No one is going to snatch her away from you. Now I'm going to earn my ridiculous fee by starting on the repairs. I can use the back entrance to bring up my equipment. Come along, you two."

Before Mganak could protest again, Emtal herded Darla and Tanik towards the back of the hold and the entrance to the engine compartment.

"I am not sure that this is a good idea," he growled.

"I'm sure it will be fine," Wanda said soothingly, hoping her own concerns didn't show. "Do you trust Emtal?"

He gave a reluctant nod. "I do. She would never have let me get away with anything and I do not believe she has changed."

"Well, there you go. Maybe we could just take a short walk?"

"It would be nice to be off the ship for a little while," Alicia added.

"Very well," he sighed, then looked at the guns they were still holding. "Better give those back and I'll lock them up."

Wanda handed hers over readily enough, but Alicia hesitated.

"I would prefer to keep it. Do you have another holster?"

Mganak regarded her thoughtfully for a moment, then retrieved a harness from the weapons cabinet. He showed her how to adjust it, and a moment later, it was fastened around her slender waist. Somehow, it looked perfectly at home there.

Only Alicia could make a gun look like a fashion accessory, Wanda thought wistfully as Mganak handed her an oversized cloak.

"What's this for?"

"To conceal your beauty," he said firmly—which was both sweet and annoying. She hesitated, then reluctantly put the cloak around her shoulders as Alicia chuckled.

Great. Alicia looks like a badass, and I look like the Pillsbury dough boy in a cloak, she thought grumpily as she prepared to exit the ship. Mganak wrapped his arm and his tail around her.

"You are as beautiful as ever, mishka." he whispered.

Somewhat appeased, she accompanied him down the ramp. They were halfway across the open floor of the dock when yet another alien appeared. Mganak immediately tensed and stepped in front of the two women.

"Rafalo," he growled.

"Mganak," the male said affably. "Nice to have you back."

"I am not back."

Wanda wasn't sure what she had expected Rafalo to look like, but it wasn't the flamboyant male standing before her now. He was dressed, well, like a pirate. Tight dark pants were tucked into black boots while a flowing white shirt was open to reveal what even she had to admit was an impressively muscled chest.

His skin appeared to be covered in short golden fur while a carefully curled mane flowed down to his shoulders. And were those horns peeking out of that mane? His features were humanoid, although his nose was flatter and his mouth wider than those of a human. The fangs glinting beneath his upper lip were also clearly not human. As he drew closer, she could see that the fur around his mouth was white and white strands threaded through the golden mane, but he was undeniably attractive.

Beside her, Alicia gave a quiet gasp. "Who's that?" she murmured.

"Rafalo. He runs the station," she responded, equally quietly.

"I do indeed." He swept a deep bow, then smiled disarmingly despite the white flash of fang. "And I should warn you that I have excellent hearing."

He took a step closer and Mganak growled again.

"Don't be ridiculous. I'm not going to hurt your females. I simply wish to be introduced. Don't you trust me?"

CHAPTER THIRTEEN

M ganak stared at Rafalo, wishing he had an easy answer to the other male's question. The last time he had seen the captain, Rafalo was being dragged off by Regtenian guards. His clothes had been ripped, one arm dangling limply, and blood had been streaked down his shirt. Mganak had been equally damaged but the pain in his body had been nothing to the pain in his heart as he watched his mentor, the male he would have once trusted with his life, condemned for a terrible crime.

"I see." As usual, Rafalo sounded bored and faintly mocking, but even after all this time, Mganak knew him all too well. He saw the brief flare of hurt in the other male's eyes before Rafalo swept another bow. "Then I shall depart."

"No. Wait." The words were out before he could call them back. "This is my ma... mishka, Wanda." Ignoring the sudden suspicion on the other male's face, he hurried on. "And this is Alicia. They are human."

"Yes, I know. Taken by Vedeckians, I assume?"

"Yes. How did you know?"

"Oh, don't look so suspicious. I have... heard rumors." Before Mganak could demand an explanation, Rafalo turned to Wanda. "I am delighted to make your acquaintance. I trust you will be comfortable on my station."

"I..." She shot Mganak an uncertain look, then smiled a little weakly at Rafalo. "Thank you. I'm sure we will be."

"And my lady Alicia. It has been a long time since such a charming female has visited my lowly abode."

"I'm sure," Alicia said coolly, but Mganak saw the hint of color beneath her dusky skin. "I hope that I will be equally pleased to have met you."

"But of course. I am as harmless as a kit."

Mganak snorted.

"All of you should dine with me tonight." The look Rafalo shot Mganak was mostly challenging, but once again there was a flash of vulnerability that made Mganak reconsider his first impulse to refuse.

"Perhaps."

"Excellent. Shall we say at 21:00?" Rafalo seemed to consider his acceptance a given and immediately turned back to Alicia. "Would you care to see more of my station?"

"We had discussed taking a look around..." Alicia gestured to Wanda.

"Both of you, of course. It would be an honor to escort two such attractive females."

"They are not going anywhere without me," he growled.

"Naturally," Rafalo said sardonically, then extended his arm to Alicia. "My lady?"

To Mganak's shock, she took it, although he noticed she brushed her hand across her weapon first. Rafalo's smile broadened as he turned to lead the way out of the dock.

Mganak sighed and tucked Wanda's hand into his own arm as he followed his former captain.

"Are you all right?" Wanda whispered.

"Fine," he said shortly, then put his tail around her waist in silent apology. It wasn't her fault that he was on edge.

His uneasiness didn't vanish as they wound their way through the utility corridors and into the main commercial area. He hadn't been here in fifteen years, and yet it all seemed so familiar, at least until they reached the market area. Had it always been this... seedy?

Pasha smoke streamed out of the numerous bars lining the narrow corridors, while blinking lights indicated an equal number of gambling establishments. Advertisements for pleasure companions flashed at regular intervals, competing with small stalls selling a variety of foods. A wide mixture of races jostled each other as they staggered from one establishment to the other, and he was quite sure that it had never been this crowded.

Wanda's eyes widened as she looked around and he was immensely grateful that she had agreed to cloak herself considering the number of looks she received in return.

Rafalo, of course, strode through the crowd without a backward look, completely unconcerned about the attention that he and the female at his side were also attracting. The crowd kept a respectful distance from the captain.

"I don't think this is exactly what I imagined," Wanda whispered. "And you grew up here?"

"Only occasionally," Rafalo responded, his keen hearing picking up the question. "We traveled frequently and only came back here a few times a year. But after my little incident on Regten, I decided that I preferred to remain someplace where I was in control."

Once again, the usual mixture of guilt and anger swept over him. He had been wrong, so wrong, but Rafalo had made no attempt to correct his mistake. You should have known better, his conscience prodded.

Still lost in thoughts of the past, he paid little attention when Rafalo turned down first one narrow passageway, then another, before finally leading the way through a nondescript doorway. Heavy shadows obscured the next corridor and only a few dim red lanterns lit the way. Wanda pressed closer to him, and his misgivings reappeared.

"Where are you taking us?" He wasn't familiar with this part of the station at all.

"Somewhere the females will enjoy," Rafalo said airily, only increasing Mganak's suspicions.

"Are you sure about this?" Wanda asked softly.

"Trust me." Rafalo's voice floated back as he turned another corner and then unlocked a door.

His hand on his holster, Mganak followed him, then stumbled to a halt so quickly that Wanda ran into him. Instead of the dark, smoke-filled halls they had passed through, they had emerged into a broad white corridor. Here too, a number of establishments lined the walls but instead of gambling dens and advertisements for pleasure companions, these were cozy restaurants and a wide variety of small, colorful stores and market stalls. There weren't as many people bustling about, but it was far from empty.

"This was not here before."

"No it wasn't." Rafalo's tail lashed rhythmically. "But I realized that not everyone appreciates the more... colorful part of the station."

Mganak still couldn't believe his eyes. This area looked as peaceful and prosperous as any of the settlements he visited. The majority of the inhabitants were male but across from him, two females were bargaining over a food purchase, and further down the corridor, he saw a richly dressed female vanishing into a doorway.

"Is there a clothing store?" Wanda asked eagerly. "Or perhaps somewhere to purchase fabric?"

"Yes, indeed." Rafalo led them down the market and into what was obviously a female dress shop.

Several people greeted him as they passed, and no one seemed disturbed by his presence. They eyed Mganak with much greater suspicion, but no one confronted him.

The owner of the dress shop greeted them cordially, and the three females were soon deep in discussion about colors and fabrics. Rafalo leaned against the counter, perfectly at ease, and smiled as he watched them.

"I do not understand," Mganak muttered.

"No, I don't suppose you do." Rafalo threw him a challenging look. "As I said, after Regten I wanted to be in control. At first I just came back here to lick my wounds and because I thought perhaps you might return."

Fuck. Another wave of guilt swept over him.

When Mganak didn't respond, Rafalo shrugged. "But eventually, I got bored here. By myself. I decided to expand the capabilities of the station."

"Were you really smuggling the slaves off of Regten?" Mganak burst out.

Rafalo sighed. "You still doubt me? Is that why you never returned? Never did more than send me that stiff formal apology?"

"I don't know. Perhaps. When I ran into Boral and he told me what had really occurred—or what you said had really occurred—it seemed like it was too late. Too much time had passed. I was better off on my own and you were better off without me."

"Was I?" Before Mganak could respond, Rafalo's eyes

widened. Mganak followed his gaze and saw that he was staring at Wanda. She had slipped off her cloak, and her lush body was all too obvious, as was the gentle swell of her stomach. "Your mate is with child?"

"I did not say that she is my mate," he said reluctantly.

"You forget how well I know you. It was obvious from the moment you emerged from the ship with her." Rafalo frowned at him. "Why would you deny it when she is carrying your child?"

"She is not my child." The words felt wrong in his mouth. The child that responded under his hand, that he felt moving when he and Wanda were pressed together, felt like his child. "Wanda was already pregnant when she was abducted by the Vedeckians."

Rafalo growled. "She is mated to another?"

"No. She chose to have a child on her own. She is very brave."

"Indeed." Rafalo regarded him thoughtfully but rather to Mganak's surprise, he didn't comment further. Instead, he changed the subject. "I suspect that they are going to be here for a while. We should go and have a drink."

Mganak cast an uneasy glance around the small shop. It seemed safe enough but...

Rafalo laughed. "There's a place across the way. We can sit outside, and you can watch anyone who enters or exits."

The idea appealed to him more than he'd expected. With a nod, he went to tell Wanda where he would be. She nodded absently as she held up a swath of pale green cloth.

"Do you think Darla would like this?"

"I think she would prefer blue. Are you sure you do not mind if I leave you?"

She laughed and finally focused on him. "In other words, you're like every other male and you don't enjoy shopping."

"I would be content to remain at your side," he said truthfully.

"No, go have a drink with your... friend. We'll be fine."

"I will be directly across the way if you need me."

She reached up and touched his cheek. "I always need you, Mganak." Then she grinned. "But maybe not while trying on clothes."

His chest ached even as he growled and pulled her closer. "As long as you need me to remove them."

He kissed her until they were both breathless and his cock strained at his pants. She was flushed and smiling when he finally let her go. Filled with satisfaction, he didn't even mind when Alicia rolled her eyes and Rafalo gave him a knowing look. As long as his mate was happy, that was all that mattered.

CHAPTER FOURTEEN

Mganak stalked back into the dress shop, his tail twitching angrily. Sitting down for a drink with Rafalo had not gone well. The other male made casual conversation about the station, but there was an underlying note of hostility and, even worse, hurt beneath his casual words. Mganak's own hurt and anger were just as close to the surface. Twice he was on the verge of demanding a full explanation, but both times he ended up backing away from the subject. What good would it do after all this time? It also didn't help that he was essentially at the mercy of Rafalo for the work he needed done on his ship. Emtal would never continue without Rafalo's permission.

At least the sight of Wanda talking to the other two females made him smile. Her cheeks were flushed, and she looked happy and excited. Her smile grew even wider as she rushed over to meet him.

"Dolai has the most marvelous things." She gestured at the shopkeeper, a tall Trevelorian female with a pink crest who bobbed her head shyly when he looked at her. "She has a beautiful little dress that will be just perfect for Kanda. Alicia and I found a few things as well. Unfortunately, she doesn't have anything readymade for the other two, but we picked out some great fabrics and I know Alicia can do a lot with them." The rush of words came to a halt and her smile turned rueful. "I hope it's not too expensive."

"I have plenty of credits," he assured her. "And I mentioned selling the lifeboat to Emtal. She does not think it will be hard to find a buyer."

"I still have to talk to Kareena," she reminded him. "But it would be a relief to be able to pay you back—"

He growled and tugged her closer to him. "The credits are for all of you. There is no debt between us. I am more than happy to provide anything that you will need."

She bit her lip, then patted his tail where it was wrapped around her waist. "I wasn't trying to insult you, Mganak. It's just that you have done so much for us already."

"And it has been my pleasure to do so." He only wished that he could do more. Who was going to take care of her and the children after they left him?

He gave her a reassuring hug and went to present his credit chip to the storekeeper, only to find Rafalo attempting to do the same thing while Alicia glared at him, her hands on her hips.

"I do not want you to pay for my purchases."

"But it would be my pleasure. You deserve only the finest to match your beauty."

"I've never taken charity from anyone, and I'm not about to start now."

"Here." Mganak passed his credit chip to Dolai, and she took it with a twinkle in her eye when Alicia didn't protest.

Rafalo gave an outraged huff. "Why do you not object to Mganak paying?"

"Because he's... family," Alicia said firmly.

A warm glow filled Mganak, and he started to smirk at

Rafalo, but then he saw the flash of hurt in the other male's eyes. They had been a family once, or at least he had thought so. But that relationship had ended, just as his first family had ended. Was he being foolish to think that he had a third chance?

Subdued, he gathered up the packages. "We should return to the ship."

"Yes of course." Rafalo didn't object but his shoulders were stiff and his normal insouciance seemed to have deserted him.

Mganak saw Alicia watching the other male thoughtfully. After thanking the shopkeeper, the four of them exited the shop, then stood uncertainly.

Alicia looked down the rest of the shopping corridor. "What other types of shops do you have here?"

"We have the finest collection of merchants in the sector," Rafalo said with an extravagant gesture, but he still seemed unduly subdued.

"Do you have a bakery or a candy store? A place that sells sweet things to eat?"

He nodded. "Narlin is very talented in that regard."

Alicia glanced at Wanda. "I think the children might enjoy a treat."

"I'm sure they would, but I think we should get back. This took longer than I expected."

After a brief hesitation, Alicia flashed Rafalo a challenging look. "Will you accompany me? That way Mganak and Wanda can return to the ship now and you can bring me back in a little while."

"But of course. It would be a pleasure to accompany you, my lady." Rafalo swept a flamboyant bow, once more his usual self. "And perhaps you would allow me to purchase the treats for the children? Not as charity but as a gift," he added hastily.

Alicia bowed her head with regal elegance, but Mganak

saw the smile playing on her lips. Wanda must have seen it as well because she hid her own smile as she tucked her arm in his and smiled at the other female. "That's all settled then. We'll meet you back at the ship."

"Here." Rafalo handed Mganak a small control. "This area of the station is off limits to everyone except those who live here. This will give you entry through the door we used if you wish to come back and make additional purchases. I assume I can rely on your discretion?"

Despite the underlying barb in the words, Mganak only nodded his head. "Of course. Come, mishka."

WANDA TUGGED NERVOUSLY AT HER NEW GOWN AND wished she had a mirror. She really needed to ask Mganak to install one for her…

No. There was no point in asking him for a mirror when she wouldn't be with him much longer. The knowledge sent a wave of desolation over her. The more time they spent together, the more she didn't want to leave him. What if she could stay with him? She put her hand over her stomach and the baby moved as if in response. What would be best for her?

And Mganak himself had still not asked her to stay with him. She was sure enough of his interest that she didn't think he would refuse if she asked, but once the initial passion between them died down, would he be happy with a ready-made human family? He had been alone for a long time and she could only assume he must have preferred it that way.

She was still frowning at that idea when he entered the cabin, and she immediately lost her train of thought. For once, he had abandoned his usual black and instead was dressed in a close-fitting white shirt that accentuated his broad, muscular chest. Equally well-fitting white pants clung to strong thighs and lovingly cupped his cock. She dragged her gaze away when she saw him jerk in response.

When she looked up at his face, he was studying her with undisguised hunger, his eyes heated.

"You look beautiful, mishka. I am torn between wishing to show you off and wishing to hide you away from everyone so that only I can appreciate your beauty."

She could feel her face flush but she did her best to ignore her embarrassment and gave a little twirl, smiling as her dress floated out around her. Even without a mirror, she knew that the pale green color suited her and she loved the way the silky fabric criss crossed her breasts before flaring out from the high Empire waist.

"I'm just glad that Dolai had something that fit me."

His tail tugged her closer. "Are you sure you still wish to have dinner with Rafalo?"

"Pretty sure." She gave him a rueful smile. "It's not as if the children missed us earlier."

They had come back from the shopping expedition to find Darla engrossed in the repairs. She and Tanik were still giving each other shyly admiring looks, but the girl seemed almost as impressed by Emtal's skills.

"Did you know that she worked on the generation ships?" Darla whispered in awe to Wanda.

"That's nice." Wanda wasn't exactly sure what the accomplishment meant, but she couldn't help feeling a little jealous of the girl's obvious admiration for the older female.

Darla laughed and gave her a quick impulsive hug. "I'm having such a good time."

"I'm glad, sweetheart." Wanda hugged her back and looked up to find Emtal watching them thoughtfully, but she didn't say anything before burying her head in the engine again. "Captain Rafalo has invited us all for dinner tonight."

"Do we have to go? I'd rather stay here and watch Emtal work."

"I'm sure Emtal will want to go home," Wanda said gently.

"Nah. At least not until after we get these crystals out." Twinkling black eyes surveyed Wanda. "I don't mind keeping an eye on the girl if she wants to stay."

"And you know Davy won't want to go," Darla added quickly. "He hates new places."

Mganak had gone to put away the purchases when they returned to the ship but he joined them in time to hear Darla's last words. "Where does Davy not want to go?"

"Darla says they'd rather stay here than go to dinner with Captain Rafalo," Wanda explained. "Emtal offered to stay with them."

"Are you sure?" Mganak frowned at the older female. "I did not think you had any experience with children."

Emtal snorted. "You weren't much more than a pup yourself when you joined us."

"I suppose it is all right." Mganak scowled at Tanik, who had been listening silently. "Is the young male going home?"

"No, my assistant is remaining to assist me," Emtal said tartly. "Which he could do more efficiently if you weren't standing around cross questioning me. Maybe I should add a surcharge to my bill for interference."

Wanda saw Mganak hide a smile as he meekly bowed his head. "Yes, Emtal."

Leaving Darla with Emtal and Tanik, they went upstairs to find Davy. He scowled and shook his head when she asked him if he wanted to go to dinner with them. Kareena also turned down the invitation. She still looked terrified at the idea of leaving the ship. She also didn't seem thrilled at the knowledge that Emtal would be remaining, but she put her hand on Sagat's head and nodded.

In the end, Alicia was the only one who decided to accompany them.

Now when Mganak carried Wanda down to the lounge, Alicia awaited them, wearing her own new dress. The coral silk sheath with a deep cowl neck suited her slender figure.

"You look amazing," Wanda said sincerely. Even when she wasn't pregnant, she had never looked that elegant.

Alicia shrugged a shoulder but a pleased smile curved her mouth. "Dolai is a very talented seamstress."

Mganak sighed as he led the way to the lift. "I am glad that Rafalo is coming to meet us. I am afraid that the two of you will draw a lot of attention."

Rafalo was waiting, his gaze immediately going to Alicia. He looked stunned—and oddly shy—before he recovered enough to give her a sweeping bow.

"You are a vision of beauty, my lady. Ladies," he added hastily. "It is my pleasure to escort two such attractive females."

"Are you sure about this?" Mganak asked.

"They will be safe with us, but perhaps it would be best if we chose another route."

Rafalo offered his arm to Alicia, and she gracefully placed her hand on his. Mganak drew Wanda closer as they fell in step behind the other couple. This time, Rafalo did not lead them into the part of the station they had seen the first time. Instead, he led them through a small door on the other side of the dock, then took them on a wandering journey through what seemed to Wanda like a maze of corridors before unlocking another door.

They emerged into the clean white section of the station again, although not in the shopping district. Directly in front of them was an unexpected expanse of greenery.

Her eyes threatened to fill with tears as she pulled Mganak

towards the small park. "It seems like such a long time since I saw things growing."

Even the air smelled fresher here with a slightly herbal note. She didn't recognize any of the plants, but it didn't matter. They were green and growing and alive—well, not entirely green. The foliage ranged in shades from gold to green to blue, but it was all lush and verdant.

Alicia also exclaimed over the park and Rafalo looked pleased.

"We have added several of these areas over the past few years. They are quite popular."

"I can certainly understand why." Alicia smiled at him.

Rafalo led them along a broad path that wound through the green area until they stopped in front of an elaborate set of double doors set in a long wall. "I am delighted to welcome you to my residence."

Behind the doors, they entered a wide courtyard, also lined with plants. Several rooms opened out onto it, and Rafalo escorted them to one set up as a dining area just as the surrounding lights began to fade. It appeared that the station had an artificial circadian rhythm as well. Small twinkling lights sprang to life throughout the courtyard.

"This is really beautiful," Wanda said sincerely and Rafalo smiled at her.

"I decided that I might as well enjoy the advantages of not being on the ship all the time."

"Have you given up *The Laughing Traveler*?" Mganak asked.

"No, but I only use it for short trips now. Alanat, Eggred, Tijkul. Places like that."

There was something deliberately provocative in his tone, and Wanda felt Mganak stiffen but he didn't respond. Rafalo studied him silently, then gestured at the table.

"Please be seated."

As Rafalo brought out dishes from a heated serving station, he explained that he had cooked the meal. The food was delicious and the setting lovely, but the underlying current of tension continued throughout the meal. Although Rafalo was an entertaining host, he kept throwing in casual remarks that Wanda didn't understand but that all too clearly bothered Mganak. Both Wanda and Alicia did their best to relieve the strain.

"That was a wonderful meal," Wanda said as dinner drew to a close, savoring the last bite of dessert. The pink, fluffy concoction melted in her mouth with a burst of cool sweetness.

"Thank you. I enjoy cooking."

"I'm afraid I'm not a very good cook. It's just as well that Mganak knows his way around the kitchen."

"I know he does. I taught him."

She could tell that Rafalo was goading Mganak again, and a stiff silence descended.

Wanda and Alicia exchanged glances, and Wanda started to push back her chair. "Maybe we should be—"

"What do you want from me, Rafalo?" Mganak burst out.

"Oh, I don't know." Rafalo swirled his wine glass, his eyes focused on Mganak. "I wanted trust but it's too late for that. Perhaps an apology?"

"I sent you an apology."

Rafalo scoffed. "'It appears I was mistaken.' That was the best you could do?"

"Trust goes both ways. You never told me what you were doing." Mganak slammed back his chair, the legs scraping against the floor with a harsh screech.

"Because I didn't want you involved!"

"That did not stop the Regtenians from arresting me, did it? And even then, you denied nothing."

"Because I thought you knew me well enough to have faith in me."

"And perhaps you destroyed that faith."

Mganak stood and stormed out of the room. Wanda started to go after him but Rafalo shook his head.

"Give him time to cool down." Rafalo's anger seemed to have vanished. He looked tired and... old.

Alicia had been watching silently from across the table, and now she reached out and put her hand over his. He stared at it for a minute, then turned his own hand over and grasped hers.

"What happened between the two of you?" Wanda asked.

"Slavery is forbidden in the Confederation," he said after a long pause. "But, as you discovered, that doesn't mean that it doesn't exist. There are far fewer people than before the Red Death, but there are also far fewer enforcers of the law and they are spread thin. And with the shortage of females..." He shrugged unhappily. "To make a long story short, Mganak found out I was smuggling slaves."

"What? How could you?" A streak of terror raced through her. She started to scramble to her feet as she saw Alicia tug uselessly on his hand.

He scowled. "Both of you stop panicking. You're as bad as he was. He never even bothered to wonder why."

Wanda gave him a suspicious look. "All right, I'll ask. Why?"

"I had a deal with the Patrol. I went in, picked up a contingent of slaves, then delivered them back to the Patrol."

"Why didn't they go in themselves?"

"I told you. They were spread thin and couldn't afford an all-out war."

"But you got caught and arrested."

"Correct. My contacts eventually managed to have me freed but Mganak was long gone."

She couldn't help feeling a wave of sympathy for the obvious hurt in his voice, but her first loyalty was to Mganak. She hated the thought that he was out there alone. "I think it's time I went after him."

"I'll wait for you here," Alicia said quietly, her hand still wrapped in Rafalo's. "But I will leave whenever you are ready."

"Thank you. I'll be back." Hopefully with Mganak at her side.

CHAPTER FIFTEEN

Mganak paced back and forth in the park area. Even the courtyard had been too confining for his anger but here the surrounding vegetation soothed him, the fragrant plants helping to calm him. The delicate fragrance of his approaching mate also helped as he finally took a deep breath.

"Hi," she said softly.

"I am sorry that I left you."

"I understand. You were upset." She leaned into him as his tail pulled her closer, and he could feel the firm swell of her stomach against his side.

"I still should not have left you."

"Do you want to talk about it?"

"Did Rafalo not tell you how dishonorably I have behaved?"

"I'd like to hear your side of the story."

He sighed, then gathered her up in his arms and carried her to a small bench nearby.

"We went to Regten to pick up a ship that Rafalo had arranged to purchase. It was a routine transaction, so only the two of us went. We closed the deal without any difficulty, and then Rafalo went to take care of some business while I got the ship ready for the journey. I was on my way to meet him when the Regtenian guards grabbed me."

It certainly wasn't the first time they had run into trouble with planetary authorities, but he hadn't expected it on such a routine trip.

"I had no idea what was going on. They called me a slave trader and a thief and beat the hell out of me."

"Oh, Mganak, no." Her hand tightened on his arm.

"I kept telling them that they were wrong and finally they dragged me back to our ship. Rafalo was already there, looking even worse than I did, and they made him open all of the storage areas."

He hadn't been able to believe it when the doors opened and revealed pale, frightened faces. Slaves. Female slaves.

"He had a dozen slaves hidden on the ship. I was... furious." *And hurt and betrayed.* "If I had not seen it with my own eyes, I never would have believed it. I asked him how he could do such a terrible thing, and he just looked at me."

"Then what happened?" she asked softly when he didn't continue.

"The Regtenians decided that I had not known about the smuggling, and they eventually let me go. I went straight to the ship and never looked back. I left him in their hands, even knowing how they would treat him."

He had told himself that he had no other choice.

"After that, I decided I was better off on my own. I made no attempt to contact Emtal or any of the other crewmembers. When I eventually heard that he was back here on the station, I thought it just confirmed the fact that he was a criminal who had managed to buy his way out."

But even so, he had been relieved that Rafalo was free.

Wanda stroked his arm. "When we were on the ship, you said you found out that you'd misjudged him. How did that happen?"

"It must have been five or six years later. I was buying supplies on Boovlin. A female I did not recognize came rushing over to me to tell me how much she appreciated what Rafalo had done. She insisted that he had managed to rescue her and other slaves from Regten."

He hadn't believed her first. Didn't want to believe her. Because if she was right, he had been wrong about the entire situation and had abandoned his captain, his mentor, his friend.

"I tried to put it out of my mind, but eventually I ran into a mutual acquaintance, and he told me that Rafalo had been working with the Patrol to smuggle slaves off of the planets that were turning a blind eye to the practice."

The familiar wave of guilt washed over him. "Even then, I did not behave with honor. I sent him a message—a *message*—because I did not have the courage to face him. He was the second family I lost, and it was my own fault."

Wanda's soft hand came up to touch his cheek. "Mganak, you aren't the only one at fault here. Rafalo didn't reach out to you either, did he?"

"No. But he was not the one at fault."

"He's the one who chose not to explain." She sighed. "Hasn't it been long enough? Why don't you come back and talk to him?"

He looked down at her face and then back at the lights twinkling from Rafalo's courtyard, like a promise of home. "You are right. As always."

"Just remember you said that."

She stayed close to his side as they crossed the short distance, and her presence gave him courage.

Rafalo was still seated at the table, sprawled casually in his chair, but he didn't look triumphant at Mganak's return. He looked... hopeful?

Mganak squeezed Wanda's hand, then went to his friend.

"I was wrong," he said simply. "I was wrong not to trust you and I was wrong not to come back and face you."

Rafalo sighed. "I should have told you."

"Yes," he agreed. "But I understand why you did not."

Rafalo stood up and extended a hand. "Friends?"

As they clasped forearms, a deep sense of satisfaction filled Mganak. He felt as if a missing part of himself had been returned to its rightful place. He looked over to see both Wanda and Alicia smiling, their eyes bright.

"This calls for a celebration," Wanda said enthusiastically. "Although I'll have to limit myself—"

The buzz of a communicator interrupted her words.

"That's Emtal's signal." Rafalo frowned as he picked up the device. "What's wrong?"

Emtal's voice was clearly audible. "The boy is... unhappy, and I can't calm him."

"Davy," Mganak said immediately. "We will return at once."

Rafalo nodded. "We'll come with you."

Mganak didn't argue. He swept Wanda up in his arms and set off at a rapid pace. Rafalo followed more slowly, adjusting to Alicia's speed.

They found Davy pacing and muttering again. Sagat prowled next to him, while Darla watched, her face tired and pale. Tanik stood next to her, his hand on her shoulder. Mganak could tell she had been crying and didn't have the heart to growl at the young male. Kareena paced with a crying Kanda, her small high-pitched cries echoing through the ship. Emtal looked both exasperated and worried.

"I didn't know what was best. Darla said not to touch him."

"She is correct. We will just keep watch until he calms. Why do you not go home now?"

"Are you sure? Is there anything I can do to help?"

"No, but thank you." His tail reached out and briefly touched the older female's hand. "We will see you in the morning."

Sharp black eyes studied him, then she nodded once. "Very well. Come on, boy. Let's leave them in peace."

Tanik hesitated, glancing at Darla. Wanda had her arm around her, and the girl gave him a watery smile. "I'll see you tomorrow."

"I will be here," Tanik promised.

Rafalo and Alicia arrived just as Emtal and Tanik left. Alicia took in the situation with one glance and went to Kareena's side. Silent tears were streaming down the Vedeckian's cheeks as she tried to comfort Kanda.

"Why don't you let me hold her while you calm yourself?" Alicia asked. "She can probably tell you're upset."

Rafalo watched in what looked like awe as Alicia quieted the crying infant. Mganak felt his own tension ease as the baby's cries finally ceased. Wanda had pulled Darla down on the lower bunk, her arm still around the girl's shoulders as they watched Sagat and Davy pace, and he went to join them.

"Did something happen?" he asked softly.

"I don't know. It might have been because there were more people around. Or because his routine changed." Darla shrugged helplessly. "But sometimes there isn't a reason."

"I know, sweetheart." Wanda's endearment for the girl rose naturally to his lips, and Darla gave him a pleased smile, then leaned into him.

"I'm pretty sure it didn't help when Kanda started crying. I'm glad I don't have a baby."

Wanda laughed, and Darla winced. "I didn't mean it like that."

"I know. I think nature designed baby's cries to make sure that they couldn't be ignored."

To his relief, now that the ship was silent, Davy began to settle down. His pace slowed, and he finally looked over to see them all sitting there watching him. He came over and climbed onto Mganak's lap, tugging on his arms.

"Hug," Davy demanded.

His heart aching, he tightened his arms around the boy as he had done after the previous incident. Wanda was holding Darla almost as tightly, and their eyes met over the girl's head. This was how it should be, he realized. Somehow he had managed to find a new family. He had lost one through his failure to act and he wasn't going to make that mistake a second time.

He would ask Wanda and the children to stay.

CHAPTER SIXTEEN

D avy fell asleep in Mganak's arms, his little face serene despite the earlier episode. Darla's eyes were heavy as well, and she didn't protest when Wanda suggested that she go to bed. As she went to the sanitary facility to get ready, Mganak lifted Davy into the upper bunk. Sagat jumped up after him, curling around the boy.

Mganak stroked the smooth scales and Sagat purred with contentment.

"I know you will watch over them," he said softly and looked up to find Wanda watching him, a smile curving her lips. "He understands me."

"I have no doubt. He's so good with Davy."

Darla came to join them, her face still tired but no longer distressed. She put her arms around his waist and hugged him. "Thank you for coming back."

"Of course. I—*we*—will always be here if you need us."

It was perhaps a reckless promise, and he saw Wanda give him a startled look, but she didn't say anything. Darla hugged her also and climbed into her bunk with a wide yawn.

"Goodnight, sweetheart," Wanda said softly as they left the room.

Alicia and Rafalo were waiting in the lounge.

"Sounds like everything is quiet now," Rafalo said.

"My guess is that they're both already asleep." Wanda looked over at Alicia. "And Kareena?"

"Also asleep, I suspect. Once Kanda calmed down, she calmed down, and they both went off to bed." Alicia pursed her lips. "I worry about the two of them. Kareena is so sensitive, and Kanda picks up on it. She needs to feel secure."

"Let me see what I can do," Rafalo suggested, then grinned when they all looked shocked. "I have some connections that may be able to help."

Mganak briefly wondered what secrets the other male was still concealing, but he had more important things on his mind right now—like being alone with his mate.

"It is time for you to leave," he announced. "We are going to bed."

"But I haven't finished my drink," Rafalo protested, his eyes laughing.

"I can see him out." Alicia also looked amused but he didn't care. He swept Wanda up in his arms, ignoring her laughing protest, and headed for the stairs.

"At last," he said as they reached their cabin and sat down with her on his lap.

"Were you anxious?" she teased, but he caught the sweet scent of her arousal.

He had been, but now that they were alone and he had her safe in his arms, he was no longer in a hurry. He wrapped his tail around her waist and pulled her closer. Her baby moved, pushing against his side, and he smiled.

"I miss the stars," Wanda said sleepily. "It'll be nice to back out in space again."

His heart pounded as he realized this was the perfect time to ask her.

"Do you mean that, mishka? Are you content on my ship?"

"Very. Why?"

"Because it is all I have to offer you." He felt her pulse increase and he hurried on. "I know it is not much, but I also have plenty of credits."

"Why..." Her hand trembled in his. "Why are you telling me this?"

"Because I want you to stay with me. All of you—Darla, Davy, the child you carry. You belong with me."

"Are you sure? I thought maybe you weren't ready for a wife and three children." Her hand went to her stomach, and he covered it with his own.

"It was not that I was not ready, but I was afraid," he admitted. "Afraid that I would end up alone again. I lost one family to plague, the second to my own foolishness."

"Are you still afraid?"

"I am terrified. But I refuse to let that stop me. I know this is not your planet and I cannot offer you a home other than the ship, but I cannot bear to let you go. I love you, Wanda."

Her eyes filled with tears. "I love you too."

"Do not cry, mishka."

"They're happy tears."

He bent his head and kissed her, exploring the silky softness of her mouth until she was wiggling restlessly in his arms. His cock ached and throbbed, but he did his best to ignore it. He wanted to savor this moment.

"I think it's time," she said breathlessly, when at last he ended the kiss.

"Time for what?" he murmured, his mouth drifting down to her neck to nibble the tender flesh, seeking the places that made her shiver with pleasure.

"I want all of you."

His cock jerked so enthusiastically he feared it would force its way through his pants.

"Are you sure, mishka?"

"Yes, very sure." Her hand came up to touch his cheek. "I want you."

"You have me."

Her smile blinded him. "But not inside me."

"Not yet. But soon."

"How soon?" she demanded.

"The longer you distract me with questions, the longer it will take."

He ran his finger along the edge of her gown, watching as her skin quivered beneath his touch.

"This is a very pretty dress, but I believe we can dispense with it now," he said, tugging it off before she could respond. His breath caught at the sight of her luscious breasts completely exposed to him. The creamy mounds were untouched by the specks of gold that covered her cheeks and chest, but when he curved his hand around one, he saw the faint pink tide sweep down to cover the pearly flesh.

"I love the way your skin changes color," he murmured. His mouth hovered just above her nipple, and he saw the tight little bud peak as his breath touched it. He couldn't resist a long, slow lick.

She gasped, her hands going to his head. "And I love the way your tongue feels on me. More. Please."

He was only too happy to oblige, teasing her with light caresses before finally pulling the taut bud deep into the heated confines of his mouth. Her back arched.

"Oh, yes."

As he lingered over the tempting swell of her breasts, his tail worked its way into the slick heat between her thighs. She

140

gasped again when he reached the swollen nub of her pleasure receptacle, her hands tightening on his shoulders. He swept slowly back and forth over the sensitive flesh until he felt her body tense, felt her shudder and cry out his name. His tail slipped easily through her wetness to probe delicately at her small entrance. Her body resisted momentarily, then opened to him, impossibly snug as he worked his tail deeper into the tight channel. He thrust slowly in and out, stretching her, preparing her to take him, waiting until she was pulling impatiently at his shoulders once more.

"Are you ready, mishka?"

She wiggled restlessly, giving him a mock frown. "I've been ready, Mganak."

He reluctantly put her down long enough to strip off his own clothes, but he couldn't take his eyes off of her as he did. She glowed like a warm flame in the dim room, warming the heart that had been cold for so long as she raised her hands to him. As he bent down over her, he saw the flicker of movement beneath the firm swell of her stomach and reconsidered. He sat instead, lifting her into his lap so she straddled him, the sweet warmth of her wet cunt sliding across his aching cock. They both groaned.

He slid her slowly up and down his shaft, coating himself in her wetness as she shivered in pleasure, before positioning her over the broad head of his cock. Fighting the impulse to immediately bury himself in that enticing haven, he very gradually began to lower her. Despite her wetness, despite the way he had stretched her with his tail, she was impossibly tight, and he had to fight for each inch as he gradually worked his way into her channel. Her breath came in rapid pants, her tiny nails digging into his skin, but she took every inch.

When at last he was buried to the root in the silken fist of her body, he bent forward, resting his forehead against hers. "Now we are one, mishka."

"Yes, my love."

They clung to each other for a long perfect moment. And then she rocked her hips and desire roared through him so quickly he felt dizzy. His restraint vanished as he dragged her back up his shaft, then down, harder and faster with each stroke. He gripped the soft fullness of her ass to pull her even more tightly against him, and she gasped, growing even hotter and wetter. Her soft cries urged him on as he lost all control. She shuddered and he felt her convulsing around him, milking his cock with each wave. Fire raced down his spine, and the base of his cock swelled, locking them together as he finally, finally came in long shuddering jets of complete ecstasy.

Although they were already locked together by his knot, he wrapped his arms around her and hugged her even tighter, unwilling to let anything separate them. A ripple crossed her stomach as the baby moved between them and he smiled.

A daughter. His daughter. And another daughter and a son rested below. He had never dreamed of such happiness.

Wanda settled into an exhausted sleep before his knot subsided. She murmured a sleepy protest when he reluctantly withdrew but immediately drifted off again. He curled up behind her, but sleep did not come as easily for him. Despite his happiness, his conscience nagged at him. Was he doing the right thing for her and the children? Was it selfish to suggest bringing up the children on the ship? He had never minded it, but he had been a lot older when he stowed away on Rafalo's ship.

Afraid that his restlessness would disturb Wanda, he slipped out of bed and decided to prepare a mug of shoko for himself. Children were not the only ones who found it soothing.

The lights were low in the lounge and he assumed everyone had gone to bed, but as he came down the stairs, he heard a startled cry. Alicia sprang to her feet, looking unusually disheveled, but before he could ask any questions, Rafalo stood up next to her. The other male met his frown with a solemn stare.

"I did not realize that anyone was still awake," Mganak said.

"Rafalo was just leaving," Alicia said quickly. "We were... talking and didn't realize it was so late."

"Very late," he agreed, watching in fascination as Alicia's usual composure deserted her.

"But he's leaving now."

"As you wish, my lady." Rafalo bowed over her hand as he raised it to his lips. "But I hope to see you tomorrow."

"I... I have sewing to do. But maybe after that..."

"I will look forward to it," Rafalo said firmly, then nodded at Mganak and departed.

"You appear to have an admirer." Mganak gave her a curious look as he headed for the galley. "Would you like some shoko?"

"No, thank you," Alicia said absently. "Is that unusual? He seems like the type with a girl in every port."

"I would not say that." He thought back over the time they had spent together. Rafalo had always been flirtatious, but he rarely got involved with a female. Mganak had never seen him as focused on one as he appeared to be with Alicia. "Admittedly, it has been a long time, but he seems different around you."

"Really? Then why didn't he..."

He thought she blushed before she shook her head and visibly drew herself together. "I believe I'll go to bed now."

"Sleep well, Alicia."

She flashed him a smile and left. He proceeded to the galley but just as he finished preparing his shoko, Rafalo reappeared.

"I thought you left. Would you like some shoko?"

Rafalo shuddered. "I don't think so. I don't suppose you have any liquor?"

Mganak silently retrieved a bottle from one of the upper cabinets. He poured a small quantity into his mug and a slightly larger amount into another glass for Rafalo. "Here you go. Now why did you come back?"

"I wish to talk to you." Despite his words, he didn't add anything else. Instead he began pacing restlessly around the lounge, his tail lashing behind him. Mganak leaned against the counter and watched him. He didn't think he had ever seen Rafalo this unsettled.

"Do you have to leave as soon as your ship is repaired?" Rafalo finally burst out.

"I promised that I would take Alicia and Kareena to the Patrol station on Ayuul."

"But you could stay here longer. It would be nice for the children to have more room to run around."

"I am not sure that the station is the best place for them. Although the inner area is better."

Rafalo stopped pacing and regarded him seriously. "Can I trust you?"

His chest ached. Once there would have been no reason for Rafalo to have to ask. Perhaps the other male had not forgiven him after all.

Rafalo must have seen his distress because he hurried on. "I asked because this is not my secret, but I'm being foolish. Of course I can trust you."

He held out his glass, and Mganak silently refilled it. "It's about Tyssia."

It was the last thing that Mganak had expected him to say. "What about it?"

"It is not actually uninhabitable. The earlier surveys were incorrect. Although the upper atmosphere is primarily nitrogen, there is sufficient oxygen on the planet surface to support life." Rafalo swirled the liquor in his glass. "In fact, there is now a fairly large colony on the surface."

"Where did they come from?"

The other male shrugged. "Different places. Some of them were seeking a new life after their planets were decimated by the Red Death. But many of them are here because they were enslaved and managed to escape."

"Why are you telling me this now?"

"Because you mentioned the children. I think they would enjoy a visit to the colony. It is really quite a pleasant environment, and they would be able to run around and meet other children."

Mganak tried to temper his immediate enthusiasm. Could this be the answer? Could he give Wanda and the children more than just life on a ship?

"Are you only telling me this because you do not wish me to leave—because you do not wish Alicia to leave?"

Rafalo's tail flicked betrayingly even though he tried to appear nonchalant. "I admit I would welcome the chance to get to know her better. But I do think you should see it for yourself."

"Perhaps so. I will discuss it with my mate." Mganak drained the last of his spiked shoko. "Do I need to escort you to the door to make sure you actually leave this time?"

Rafalo laughed and shook his head. "Don't worry. I'm leaving—but I suspect that I will be returning quite early tomorrow."

"I will look forward to it," Mganak said sincerely, then

grinned. "But I hope Alicia understands what she is letting herself in for if she... spends time with you."

"I have no doubt that you will inform her—but perhaps you don't have to tell her everything."

"Perhaps not. Until tomorrow, my friend."

Rafalo reached out and clasped his hand before disappearing down the hallway a second time. Mganak smiled to himself, filled with contentment as he washed the two glasses before climbing back upstairs to where his mate waited.

CHAPTER SEVENTEEN

Wanda woke up feeling happy, lazy, and just a tiny bit sore. Mganak's massive cock had stretched her to her limit, but nothing had ever felt as good as the small nubs that covered it awakening every sensitive nerve ending. She shivered with pleasure at the memory, her nipples tightening into hard peaks.

"Good morning, mishka." Mganak was curled around her, his hand cupping her breast, and he lazily rolled the tight little bud.

"A very good morning." She wiggled around until she could smile up at him.

He bent down and kissed her, so sweetly that tears sprang to her eyes. When he lifted his head and saw the tears, he tensed. "Are you having doubts?"

"Not at all. At least not for myself or the baby..."

Alarm flickered across his face. "But?"

"But we will need to ask Darla and Davy. We can't just assume they would rather stay with us than go back to Earth."

His face relaxed. "You are right, of course, mishka, but I am sure that they will want to stay."

"How do you know?"

"Darla told Emtal and Emtal told me," he said triumphantly.

"Oh, thank goodness." She returned his smile. "Then there's only one last thing to worry about."

"And what is that, my mate?"

"Whether every time will be as amazing as the first time..."

His eyes heated as his thumb began circling her nipple. "Of course it will."

And he proceeded to prove it.

THE SECOND TIME SHE AWOKE, MGANAK WAS NO LONGER beside her, but she was far too happy and content to worry about it. She stretched lazily then made her way to the shower, walking a little gingerly as she crossed the room.

After she dressed, she went to the top of the stairs, then paused.

"Mganak?" she called softly.

Alicia came over and smiled up at her. "He's down below. Do you need him?"

"He seems to think so, but really I'm quite capable of coming down the stairs by myself. And I'm hungry."

"How about a compromise? I'll come and escort you down. That way you can tell him you had help."

"Deal!"

"You certainly look happy this morning," Alicia said after she helped her down, and Wanda felt herself blush.

"What about you? How's puss in boots?" she teased.

Alicia frowned. "More like the cowardly lion. I know he's

attracted to me, and he talks a good game, but he hasn't laid a hand on me."

"Do you want him to?"

"More than anything," the other woman said softly. "I know it's just a short-term thing, but I haven't felt this way in a very long time."

"About that... Mganak asked me to stay here with him."

"I can't say I'm surprised. He obviously loves you. Is it what you want?"

"Oh, yes."

"But what about the children?"

"We'll have to talk to them, of course, but he wants them to stay as well. And so do I."

Desolation flashed across Alicia's face, but she masked it quickly.

"Do you think it's what's best for them?"

"I think so. Mganak will be a wonderful father. But we plan to ask them this morning if that's what they want."

"I'm sure they will want to stay with you." Alicia's smile looked strained.

"Are you sure you don't want to stay too?" Wanda asked impulsively. "I'm sure you have a wonderful life back on Earth, but you don't really have a family there."

"What would I do? If I stayed?" Alicia said slowly.

"Be part of our family." She reached out and took the other woman's hand. "You already are, you know."

Alicia's dark eyes filled with tears, but she didn't let them fall. "I... I will have to think about it."

"Of course. But I hope you decide to stay."

Kareena came to join them, and Alicia eagerly reached for the baby. Kanda settled happily into her arms.

"You're so good with her," Kareena said enviously.

Wanda patted her hand. "You are too. You were just over-whelmed last night. It happens to all new mothers."

"If you say so. I'm just... afraid."

"Don't you feel safe with us?" Wanda asked. "Mganak would never let anything happen to you."

"I'm sure the captain is a great warrior, but he won't always be around. I am afraid that my... that Captain Kane will come after me."

"He isn't going to know where you are. And once we get you to the Patrol, won't they be able to return you to your family?"

Kareena shuddered. "I hope not. It is because of them that I ended up with Captain Kane. It was... arranged by them. I hope they didn't know he was planning to sell my children, but I doubt they would have cared. And as for the Patrol..." Her pretty mouth drooped. "They don't think much of Vedeckians."

Alicia looked up from Kanda long enough to raise an eyebrow at Wanda. Wanda bit her lip. It did feel like Kareena and Kanda were part of their family too, but she couldn't just keep filling up the ship with people. Could she?

"Let me talk to Mganak and see if he has any other suggestions," she offered, relieved when Kareena's face light-ened. "And speak of the devil..."

Mganak appeared in the doorway. His initial smile dissolved into a worried frown. "How did you get down here?"

She rolled her eyes. "I'm quite capable of managing a flight of stairs."

He put his arm around her, his tail curving around her stomach. "I cannot stand the thought of anything happening to you or our daughter."

The other two women sighed and Wanda relented. "Alicia helped me. Not that I needed help."

"But you will take it," he said firmly, then bent his head and kissed away any possible arguments.

By the time he lifted his head, her cheeks were glowing and she carefully avoided looking at Alicia. Instead, she changed the subject. "Are the mechanics hard at work?"

"Not yet. Emtal sent word that she needs some additional equipment. Darla is extremely disappointed." He smiled down at her. "Perhaps we could give her something else to think about."

She nodded just as the girl shuffled into the room, Davy and Sagat trailing behind her. Her lower lip poked out as she frowned at everyone.

"Good morning, Darla," Wanda said cheerfully. "Good morning, Davy." Sagat prowled over and pushed his head under her hand. She laughed and scratched along the base of his head spikes. "Good morning to you too, Sagat."

"Not that good a morning," Darla sighed. "Emtal and Tanik went off without me."

"They will be back," Mganak reminded her. "And we would like to talk to you."

"That's my cue." Alicia turned to Kareena. "Let's go try that outfit on Kanda."

Kareena cast a speculative glance at the four of them but nodded agreeably and went with Alicia.

"What's wrong?" Darla burst out.

"Nothing, sweetheart. We just wanted to talk to you and Davy." Wanda led the way to the couch.

Davy followed them, but instead of sitting down, he started stacking and unstacking his collection of plastic plates.

"Am I in trouble?" Darla's gaze cut from Wanda to Mganak.

"No, you're not. It's just... Mganak has asked me to be his mate and to stay with him."

Darla's lip trembled but she nodded. "I'm glad, even though we'll miss you."

"You do not have to miss her." Mganak put his hand on Darla's shoulder. "We want both of you to stay with us."

The desperate hope lighting up Darla's face was hard to watch. "You mean adopt us? Be our Mom and Dad?"

"Yes, sweetheart," Wanda said softly. "If that's what you want?"

"Yes!" The girl threw herself first at Mganak, then at Wanda, her thin arms almost painfully tight. "Did you hear that, Davy? This is going to be so cool. We can stay on the ship forever and Mganak will teach me how to be a mechanic and we never have to go to another lousy foster home."

Davy looked up from his plates, his eyes going from Wanda to Mganak, then he nodded firmly. "Stay," he agreed.

"But perhaps not on the ship forever." Mganak drew Darla against his side. "Although I will teach you everything I know, we may have another home."

"Where?" Wanda and Darla spoke simultaneously.

"I did not get a chance to tell you this morning, mishka, before you distracted me, but Rafalo mentioned last night that there is a colony on the planet below. It might be a good spot to build a home."

Darla frowned. "But I like the ship."

"I am not getting rid of it," he assured her. "But would it not be nice to have a house? And a room of your own?"

"Do I get to choose the color?" she asked suspiciously, and he laughed.

"As long as Wanda—as long as your mother approves."

"I'd like my own room. And we'd be close enough to visit Emtal and Tanik."

"To visit Emtal," Mganak growled, and both Wanda and Darla laughed.

"Okay. I'm in. Mom." The girl threw her arms around Wanda's neck again, and Wanda drew her close. A small hand clutched her knee, and she looked down to see Davy leaning against her. Mganak's tail wrapped around them all, and she smiled at him.

"A house? Really?"

"Yes, mishka."

"In that case—"

Before she could ask him if there would be room for Alicia and Kareena and Kanda, footsteps came thudding down the hallway. She looked over in time to see Rafalo racing into the room, a Vedeckian at his side.

CHAPTER EIGHTEEN

Mganak snarled at the sight of the Vedeckian, leaping to his feet and stepping in front of his family.

"Where is Alicia?" Rafalo demanded.

"Why? And why is he here?"

"Kwaret is a friend. He came to warn us."

"Warn us of what?"

"Captain Kane is on his way to retrieve his cargo," Kwaret said quietly.

"No!" The horrified cry came from Kareena as she and Alicia joined them. She clutched Kanda to her chest, her eyes wild. "He can't have her. He can't."

"He won't," Rafalo said quickly. "But you must go with Kwaret now. He will hide you. Mganak, you stay with me."

"Mganak?" Wanda kept her voice low, but her face was equally terrified as she gathered the children close. "I don't want to lose you."

"You won't." Rafalo took a step towards her, halting when Mganak growled again. "Trust me, Mganak. This is the only way."

He knew he had been wrong before, but what if he was wrong this time? The lives of his family were at stake. How could he send them off with a strange Vedeckian?

"Please," Rafalo said urgently. "We must hide them."

Trust in him, he reminded himself. He could trust his friend.

"Go with the Vedeckian," he told Wanda. "I will come for you as soon as it is safe."

Her face was so pale that he could count each golden speck, but she nodded and put her arms around the children. "Let's go."

The whole party headed down to the cargo hold, then Kwaret led the women and children to the small secondary airlock at the rear of the ship. Silent pink tears dripped down Kareena's cheeks, but she held her head high, gently rocking Kanda in her arms. Davy threatened to balk, but Alicia managed to distract him by beginning a story. Darla flung her arms around his waist before heading after her brother. Wanda was the last to leave, and he had to forcibly pull his tail from around her wrist. She went up on tiptoes to press a quick kiss to his lips.

"I love you," she whispered, and then she was gone.

"Now what?" he asked Rafalo.

"Now we try and convince the Vedeckians that they have already been sold."

"What if they do not believe us?"

"Then we buy them time to escape," Rafalo said grimly.

It didn't sound like much of a plan, but Mganak couldn't think of another option. He unlocked the weapons cabinet and buckled on his blaster. "We will stop them."

They had just reached the bottom of the ramp when the main doors to the dock were flung open. A Vedeckian captain stalked through the opening with two, no, four, crewmembers accompanying him.

In spite of the fact that they were outnumbered, Rafalo greeted them with his usual mocking arrogance.

"Why, Captain Kane. What an unexpected pleasure. Do you have product to sell?"

Mganak did his best to hide his reaction. Was Rafalo dealing with these Vedeckians on a regular basis?

"No, I have product to retrieve." The captain's voice was just as arrogant and twice as cold, but Rafalo only shrugged.

"I'm afraid I can't help you there. I have nothing to sell at the current time."

"I am not a fool, Rafalo. Do not play games with me. This ship retrieved a lifeboat—*my* lifeboat—with *my* product on board."

"Is this true?" Rafalo asked Mganak. He sounded genuinely shocked.

Since the Vedeckians had tracked the signal, there was no point denying it. He shrugged. "I retrieved the lifeboat. However, the occupants were already dead, so I jettisoned the bodies. I kept the lifeboat to sell."

"I do not believe you," Kane snapped.

He shrugged again. "I have no intention of trying to convince you."

The Vedeckian captain's red eyes gleamed maliciously. "If your story is true, why did you not respond to my attempts to contact you?"

He stared at the other male with deliberate contempt. "I do not communicate with slavers."

Kane sneered. "Is that why you're standing next to one?"

Once again, Mganak barely managed to conceal his reaction. Was Rafalo really as innocent as he claimed? Mganak remembered the outer area of the station—the gaming establish-

ments and the multiple advertisements for pleasure companions. It was the type of place that would attract a slave trader.

Trust, he reminded himself.

"I am also standing in the same space as you," he pointed
out. "I do not enjoy either."

"Then why are you here?"

"Because of the damage you inflicted on my ship."

Kane smiled, a slow, cruel smile. "I thought we hit you. But
this is a pointless discussion. I know that you took my product,
and I know that it is here on the station."

"I am shocked that you would make such a baseless allega-
tion," Rafalo said. "Are you accusing me of lying?"

He sounded genuinely outraged.

"Yes." Kane pulled out a small device with a blinking red
light. "I always tag my property."

"Your property?" Mganak growled, anger roaring through
him at the idea that this despicable male had dared to plant a
tracker on his mate.

"My property. How fortunate that I sent her off with the
product." Kane gave them a mocking grin. "Now I can retrieve
all of them at once."

"I have no idea what you're talking about," Rafalo sighed,
sounding completely bored. "Property? Product? Just what
exactly are you missing?"

"Both. My mate is my property." Kane flashed the device
again, and Mganak stiffened.

Kareena? It had to be her. "Your mate?"

"Yes. It appears that she did not learn her lesson when I put
her with the other slaves." Kane's smile was so cold that a chill
ran down Mganak's spine. "I will have to find a more effective
lesson. But that is a personal matter. I am more interested in the
very expensive product that you have stolen from me. If it is not

returned immediately, I will make sure that no more of these profitable deals make their way to your station, Rafalo."

"You're right." Rafalo's voice turned so hard that Mganak barely recognized it. "Product theft cannot be allowed."

He heard the distinctive hum of a blaster charging and turned to find Rafalo pointing his weapon at him. The pain of the other male's betrayal was nothing compared to the pain of realizing that he had sent his family into the arms of a slaver.

He tensed, his hand hovering over his own weapon. It might be a futile attempt, but he would do his best to take out the male who had betrayed him. But even as his hand lowered to his weapon, doubts began to race through his mind.

He had told Rafalo that he trusted him. What if his friend was only acting?

That thought cut through his anger and he studied the other male more closely. Rafalo's left hand, the hand hidden from the Vedeckians, was tapping against his thigh with first one finger, then another. He was counting. Mganak met Rafalo's eyes and saw the flash of relief when Rafalo realized he'd gotten the message.

Mganak was a good shot and Rafalo even better, but they were outnumbered. Even if each of them was lucky enough to take out two Vedeckians, at least one would remain. The odds of their survival did not look good. But if it would buy Wanda and the children a chance to escape, it would be worth it.

His hand still hovering over his weapon, he nodded. Rafalo tapped his fingers again, counting down, and as the final digit met his thigh, he whirled and fired at the Vedeckians. Mganak was only seconds behind him. He aimed first at the tracking device, smiling with grim satisfaction when it exploded in Kane's hand. Blood spurted from the wounded hand, but Mganak had already turned his weapon to the next male. The

Vedeckian collapsed, but as Mganak aimed at the next, he knew that he would not be fast enough.

To his shock, before the Vedeckian could fire, a small hole appeared between his eyes and the male fell silently to the ground.

All of the Vedeckians were down, and Mganak searched frantically for the source of the shot, for another enemy.

"You'd better not shoot me, boy." Emtal's familiar cackle sounded before she stepped out from behind one of those loading machines.

"Or me." Alicia came around the corner of the ship, her gun in her hand.

And then Wanda was there, running towards him, and he forgot everything else.

WANDA THREW HERSELF INTO MGANAK'S ARMS, TEARS streaming down her cheeks as he frantically checked her body for wounds.

"What are you doing here?" he demanded. "You could have been caught in the crossfire."

"Don't worry." The tears were still falling but she managed a tremulous smile. "I stayed way back until Alicia gave the all clear."

"You were supposed to be escaping, mishka."

"I know. And Kwaret has the children safely hidden. But Alicia insisted on coming back and I couldn't let her go alone."

"You most certainly could have."

"I couldn't. And... I couldn't stand not knowing if you were safe."

He sighed heavily. "Oh, mishka. What am I going to do with you?"

"Love me?" she suggested.

"Always." He started to pull her into his arms, but then he looked over her shoulder and she saw his face tense. "Oh no. Rafalo."

Keeping his tail firmly around her waist, he led the way to where Alicia was kneeling next to a fallen Rafalo. She had her fingers tangled in his mane as she whispered frantically. "Don't you dare leave me. You promised me last night that you would be around, and by God, you are going to be here by my side."

Wanda watched in horror as Rafalo's big chest rose and fell in a long gasping breath. Red stained the left side of his body, obscenely bright against the white of his shirt. Emtal crouched next to his wounded side, pressing a wad of fabric against the injury.

He gave another shuddering breath, and then his body went still.

Tears slipped down Alicia's cheeks. "No," she whispered.

"Stop that." Emtal scowled and pressed the fabric harder against the wound.

Rafalo roared and his eyes popped open. The expression on Alicia's face was an almost comical combination of rage and relief. "You were faking?"

"No," he muttered. "I have a hole the size of a boulder in my side."

"Then why wouldn't you talk to me?"

His grin was a pale shadow of his usual charming smile. "I liked what you were saying. I'm not going to leave you, Alicia."

"You're lucky I'm not leaving," she muttered but her hand returned to his mane, stroking the tangled strands.

"When did you get here, Emtal?" Mganak asked.

The older female sniffed. "In time to see that you were about to make another foolish mistake. Fortunately, you didn't go through with it."

Mganak sighed. "You're never going to let me forget that, are you?"

"Nope." She nodded over his shoulder. "More visitors. This is turning into a regular party."

Mganak turned in that direction, and Wanda felt his body tense at the sight of another Vedeckian, then relax as he recognized Kwaret, Kareena following slowly behind him.

"Kareena?" Wanda frowned at her. "Where are the children? Is something wrong?"

"They're safe. I left them with the one who makes sweets, and Sagat is watching over them," Kareena said almost absently, her eyes focused on one of the Vedeckian's bodies. "Is he really dead?"

"Yes." Mganak's voice was grim. "He said you were his mate."

Kareena looked down at her hands. "He was, although I had no choice in the matter."

"Why didn't you tell us?" Wanda asked.

"I know I should have told you. At first I was afraid that you would reject me because of my connection to him." Her fingers twisted nervously. "And then I was ashamed that I had lied. But I should have said something. It's my fault that he came looking for us."

"It was not your fault," Mganak said gently. "He wanted the rest of you just as much."

"Or more," Kareena said bitterly. "I was never more than a trophy to him."

"Then he was a fool," Kwaret said firmly. "He should have treated you as the precious female that you are."

Wanda watched in fascination as a faint hint of pink touched Kareena's cheeks, and she gave Kwaret a shy smile.

"I am afraid that he also implanted you with a tracker,"

Mganak added. "You should have it removed as soon as possible."

Kareena shuddered and nodded.

"If you would permit me to make the arrangements?" Kwaret offered.

"Yes, please."

Two new males appeared and, at Emtal's direction, carefully lifted Rafalo onto a stretcher. Alicia hovered anxiously, then shot Wanda a worried look.

"I'm going to go with him, if that's all right? Will you be okay?"

"I'm fine," she insisted, even though her legs were beginning to feel shaky. "Let us know how it goes."

Alicia nodded and hurried off with the stretcher.

"I need to get back to Kanda," Kareena said softly. "Are you coming?"

"Not yet," Mganak said before Wanda could respond. "Tell the children we will join them shortly."

"I will accompany you," Kwaret insisted.

The two of them left and they were alone. Wanda frowned up at Mganak. "Why did you want to wait?"

"Because now you are mine," he growled and swooped her up in his arms.

CHAPTER NINETEEN

Wanda clung to Mganak as he stalked into the ship with her. His normally hard chest felt like iron, and his face was set in fierce lines. He looked like a warrior carrying off the spoils of victory, and an unexpected wave of desire swept over her.

"Mganak?" she asked uncertainly. "Is something wrong?"

"I thought I was going to die. And then to find out that you had been so close to the battle." He shuddered. "I need you, mishka."

As soon as they were inside the ship, he placed her on her feet and yanked her dress up over her head. She shivered, but not from cold. The hunger in his eyes as he surveyed her naked body sent sparks of excitement straight to her core. Being completely naked while he was still fully dressed only added to the erotic thrill.

"So beautiful," he muttered and then he was on her.

To her dazed mind, it seemed as if he was everywhere. His mouth, his hands, his tail. He licked and caressed and plucked hungrily at every sensitive inch of her body but it didn't seem to be enough for him. He growled impatiently, then turned her to face one of the mesh cages.

"Hold on," he ordered, and just as her fingers closed around the bars, he surged into her with one long hard thrust. Despite her excitement, she wasn't quite ready, and her body struggled to take him as he filled her completely. But then his hand curved around and found her aching clit and the stretching pressure exploded into pleasure.

He groaned approvingly as her body dampened, the slickness easing his way. His fingers worked feverishly at her clit while his other hand came up to tease her breasts. A fast, hard climax swept over her, but he didn't even pause. His tail slid through the increasing wetness between her legs, then circled around to probe at her back entrance. No one had ever touched her there, but the slippery intrusion only heightened her pleasure in the moment.

He felt even larger now but she wanted more, trying to push back and meet his thrusts even as he held her easily in place. His hand left her breasts and came up to trace her lips. She licked the thick digit, then sucked his finger into her mouth. He surrounded her completely, filled her completely, and she soared into a seemingly endless orgasm, wave after wave of pleasure rolling through her body as she felt him thrust deep and hold, the base of his cock expanding, locking them together in mutual ecstasy.

Carefully supporting her, he sank to the floor with an exhausted sigh. He cradled her against him and dropped kisses along the sensitive curve of her neck and shoulder.

"Do you feel better now?" she asked when she was capable of talking.

"Much," he mumbled into her neck. "Do not ever scare me like that again."

"That goes both ways. No more gunfights."

"Agreed. We will have a peaceful life from now on."

"I'm not sure that it's possible with three children," she said dryly. "Can we go and get Darla and Davy now?"

"As soon as my body releases," he promised. "I love you, mishka."

"I love you too." She sighed happily and nestled into his arms as she waited for their bodies to unlock so they could rejoin their family.

Alicia looked up and smiled when they entered Rafalo's room the next morning. She came over and hugged Wanda, then whispered in her ear. "Thank goodness you're here. He's the worst patient ever."

"I most certainly am not," Rafalo growled and Alicia jumped guiltily. "I just see no reason to remain in this bed."

"I keep forgetting how well you can hear. But you're the one who said you had a hole the size of a boulder in your side," Alicia reminded him. "While you were pretending that you were dying."

Despite the calm tone, Wanda saw the flicker of remembered fear on Alicia's face. Rafalo must have seen it too because he held out his hand to her. "I will try to do better, my lady."

"You'd better," she muttered but she returned to her post at his side and took his hand.

Rafalo grinned at Mganak. "I assume you have questions?"

"You know I do." Mganak scowled at his friend, and Wanda gave his tail a soothing pat.

Even though the battle had been successful, she knew that he was still troubled by Rafalo's apparent familiarity with the Vedeckian slave traders. He had speculated about it for a good portion of the previous evening until she finally took his hand

and took him off to bed. At least that had put an end to his questions.

"Why did you know those males?" Mganak burst out.

"I told you that I had decided to exert more control over my circumstances, but that didn't mean I wanted to stop helping slaves escape. I'm still working with the Patrol." Rafalo shrugged. "You've seen the outer part of the station. It's a perfect front. Sometimes I arrange to purchase the slaves directly and then free them. Other times, I advise the Patrol, and they will pick up the ship after it leaves."

Mganak sighed and sat in the visitor's chair, pulling Wanda down on his lap. "You could have told me."

"I had every intention of doing so, but the situation escalated before I had a chance."

"And what about Kwaret? Where does he fit in?"

"He has been trying to help ever since..." Rafalo looked at Alicia and then at Wanda. "He was part of the crew of one of the first Vedeckian ships to travel to Earth. He became friends with one of the humans and decided to do what he could to help."

A sick feeling swept over her, even though she wasn't entirely surprised. "You mean we weren't the first to be taken?"

Rafalo shook his head. "Kwaret is aware of at least three other instances, but we suspect it could be many more."

"What happened to those women?" Wanda asked, her stomach churning. "Assuming that they were women."

"They were." Rafalo frowned. "The Vedeckians intended to sell them as breeders because of the shortage of females after the Red Death. But now it seems as if they have branched out."

"Two of the guards were talking about that—that there could be a demand for different types of slaves."

Mganak and Rafalo exchanged glances before Rafalo continued. "I am afraid the situation is only going to get worse.

I have suggested that the Patrol keep a closer watch on Earth, but if the word is out that it is an easy target..."

It was a terrible thought. Wanda could only hope that the Patrol was successful.

"What happened to the other human women? The ones who were taken before?" Alicia asked.

"Most of them ended up mated and chose to remain." Rafalo's expression lightened, and he raised an eyebrow at Mganak. "It appears that human females are quite attracted to Cire males."

"Not all of them," Alicia said tartly.

Rafalo's hand closed over hers. "And thank Hebra for that."

Wanda replayed his words in her mind. "You said most of them. What about the others?"

"The Patrol returned them to Earth—with their memories wiped."

She recoiled in horror. It would have been terrible not to be able to remember the time she had spent with Mganak, and with the others. Thank goodness she was staying.

"Why would they do that?" Alicia asked.

"It is forbidden to provide knowledge of our civilization to pre-spaceflight planets. The Confederation does not want to interfere in another planet's development."

"I suppose that makes sense," Wanda admitted reluctantly. "But I'm glad that it won't happen to me."

"Me too," Alicia agreed. "So what happens now?"

Rafalo smiled at her. "Now we all live happily ever after."

Wanda laughed with the others, but curled up in Mganak's lap, his arms snug around her, she couldn't help but think that Rafalo had only spoken the truth.

CHAPTER TWENTY

"I can't see anything yet!" Darla bounced excitedly from one side of the small flyer to the other, peering through the windows, while Davy refused to look up and concentrated on his tool instead.

Mganak had borrowed the flyer in order to take them down to Tyssia. After discussing it with Rafalo, he had decided to leave *The Wanderer* on the station for now. His friend had explained that they tried to keep traffic to the planet as discreet as possible.

Only the four of them, plus Sagat, were on board. Kareena had remained behind so that Kwaret would assist her with filling out the documentation associated with her former mate's death. Under Vedeckian law, she was entitled to a percentage of his holdings. By signing over that percentage to Kane's family, Kwaret thought that they wouldn't make any claim on her. The information would be sent from a distant location, and the Patrol had already picked up the rest of the crew. There should be nothing that would lead back to Kareena.

Alicia too had remained behind, unwilling to leave Rafalo

even though he was already recovering his strength. The two had been inseparable since the shooting. Mganak couldn't blame her—nothing would have taken him from Wanda's side if she had been injured. The thought of how close she had been to the battle still made his heart race. She patted his tail soothingly, and he realized that it was clutching at her wrist.

He gave her an apologetic smile. "Are you ready to see our new home?"

"Are you sure about this?" she asked softly. "I know how much you love *The Wanderer*."

"It is not going anywhere. I thought perhaps we could travel to Trevelor once the baby is born."

"It would be nice to meet the other women," she agreed. "But as long as I have my family, I'm happy."

He squeezed her wrist again and turned back to the controls. The vessel dropped through the last layer of wispy pink clouds, and they could finally see the ground below.

"It's so pretty," Darla said uncertainly. "It doesn't look like the kind of place that needs a mechanic."

He laughed. "Rafalo assured me that there is much work to be done."

His initial plan had been to continue with his salvage operations, but Rafalo had pointed out that it would be challenging with his family along. Instead, he had suggested that Mganak concentrate on smaller repairs. In addition to the needs of the settlement, Rafalo had plenty of work for him to do. And if he needed to work on a larger piece or to take advantage of the station's facilities, it would be an easy commute. After discussing it with Wanda, he had agreed. Darla had not been as easy to convince.

"It is pretty," Wanda agreed.

Gently rolling hills were lush with plant life in colors ranging from green to gold to blue, and he realized that the planet must have been the source for Rafalo's park. A meandering purple river ran along the base of the hills, and he followed it until a small town came into sight.

"Cheelin up ahead," he announced, and Darla came to peer over his shoulder and look at the town. Even Davy abandoned his tool and joined them.

A neat grid of streets comprised the center of the town, but as the streets extended out past the town boundaries, they began to curve and follow the landscape instead. Rafalo had arranged for them to take over a larger house at the edge of town. The farmer who had occupied it previously moved to another village in pursuit of a female. Rafalo had purchased the house and land from him before deciding that he did not want to leave the station.

"If you like it, I'll sell it to you for a very reasonable price," Rafalo had said, his eyes twinkling.

"I am sure you will. What is wrong with it?"

"Not a thing." When Mganak raised a skeptical brow, Rafalo laughed and shrugged. "It's structurally sound but has not been lived in for several years. It could use some... maintenance."

Now as the flyer descended towards the property, Mganak realized that Rafalo had understated the matter. Built from blocks of white stones, the house must have been quite impressive at one time. A wing extended on each side of a central courtyard that at one time had contained a fountain. The structure still remained, but the basin was choked with weeds. More weeds sprang from the roof of the house and poked out of numerous cracks in the facade.

"Rafalo said it needed work. He didn't say how much." He gave Wanda an apologetic look, but to his surprise, she didn't look disappointed.

"I don't think it's as bad as it looks," she said cheerfully. "It's certainly big enough, and look at all those windows. Based on how tall they are, the ceilings must be high as well."

He had to admit that the house had a certain faded elegance. It was also located on a beautiful piece of property, and he saw several outbuildings that would be perfect for his workshops. He brought the flyer to a landing just outside the courtyard and lifted her out. The children jumped down and immediately raced off to explore, Sagat in tow. In spite of his doubts about the house, they looked so happy he knew he was going to be making that excellent deal with Rafalo.

Wanda tugged him eagerly through the house, throwing open windows and exclaiming with delight.

"I was right. Look how big these rooms are! And the tile floors are gorgeous."

"Really?" He frowned at the dusty surfaces.

"They just need to be cleaned."

And the peeling paper stripped from the walls and the windows repaired. He sighed heavily. At least the few items of furniture that remained, massive wooden pieces, were in good condition underneath the dirt.

Wanda kept trying to dart ahead of him, and once he realized that the structure was basically sound, he stopped trying to restrain her. She danced eagerly from room to room, calling out her finds as she went. He followed more slowly, adding new items to the ever-increasing list of work which needed to be done.

"Mganak!" she cried suddenly, and he raced after her.

"What is it? What's wrong?"

"Nothing's wrong. But this room—isn't it perfect for our bedroom?"

As his heart quit racing, he took a look around and decided that she was right. A small connected room to the left would be perfect for the baby, and he could see a large bathroom—in desperate need of repair—off to the right. Tall glass doors lined the other two sides of the room. One set opened onto a small terrace covered with an arbor of overgrown flowering vines. The others opened onto a balcony that looked out over the entire valley.

"Do you think we will be able to see the stars from here?" Wanda asked softly as she came to join him on the balcony.

"I do not know if we will be able to see through the clouds." From the ground they simply appeared as a pale pink sky far overhead. "But we will know that they are there."

He heard laughter from below and looked down to see Darla and Davy chasing each other through a field of flowering grasses, Sagat slinking along behind them.

His tail wrapped around Wanda's waist as he pulled her closer. "Thank you, mishka."

"For what?" She smiled up at him.

"For giving me all this. A home. A family. Love."

"You're giving them to me as well."

But he suspected that he had needed them far more and he would never stop being thankful.

"WANDA," MGANAK CALLED AS HE ENTERED THEIR HOUSE four months later. It had been a busy time, but their hard work had paid off. The house had been restored to its original glory, and the big, open rooms were perfect for their family.

"I'm in the bedroom."

This room too had undergone a dramatic transformation, but he barely noticed, all of his attention focused on his beautiful, naked mate. She was close to her due date, and her body was all lush, ripe curves, glowing in the warm afternoon sun. His cock immediately sprang to a full, aching erection.

"You are naked."

"And you're very observant."

"Why?" he growled, prowling toward her.

"The children are with Alicia, and my back aches. I was hoping you could... distract me."

"Are you sure?" he asked, despite the urgency building in his cock.

"Very sure." She cupped her breasts, the heavy mounds overflowing her small hands as she offered them to him.

He groaned and lifted her into his arms, carrying her to the bed. The big wooden frame was at the perfect height, and he rubbed his still-clothed cock against her hot, wet cunt as he bent down to lick a dark, swollen nipple. A drop of milk beaded on the tip, and he sucked eagerly as she pressed against him. He could feel her getting hotter, wetter, and he impatiently freed his erection. He slid his cock through her folds, letting the nubbed surface tease the sensitive flesh and pressing harder each time he rubbed against her clit. She arched against him as he sucked harder and his tail worked its way into her tight channel. He felt her fluttering around him as she came, calling out his name.

"How does your back feel now?" he murmured.

"Ready for more."

He laughed and gave her what she wanted.

WANDA GAVE HIM A RUEFUL SMILE WHEN HIS KNOT finally subsided and he reluctantly pulled free. "I can't wait until we don't have all of this between us."

Her hand curved over her stomach and he covered it with his own. "It makes no difference to me," he said. "This is just a visible reminder that you have made me part of a family again."

"You say the sweetest things." Her eyes filled with the tears that came all too readily these days. "I love you, Mganak."

"I love you too, mishka. Now wait here while I fetch a cleansing cloth."

"I'm pretty sure I'm not going anywhere without help. Or a crane," she muttered, but she was smiling again.

After he attended to her, he helped her sit up, then dropped a loose gown over her head before carefully lifting her to her feet, steadying her with his tail until she adjusted. She put a hand on her back and winced. "You made me forget about my backache for a little while, but it's returned with a vengeance."

"Is there anything I can do to assist?"

"Not unless you can carry this baby. But maybe a little exercise will help. Do you want to walk me around the garden?"

"Of course." He suspected they wouldn't get any further than the comfortable chairs he had placed beneath the flowering arbor, but he would do whatever he could to accommodate her. Barig, the local midwife, had warned them that the baby could arrive at any time, and he was not going to leave her side.

They only made it three steps before she froze and clutched his arm.

"What is wrong—"

A splash of liquid hit his calf and he looked down to see a spreading puddle beneath her.

"I think my water just broke."

Her voice sounded oddly calm, but panic and guilt immediately raced through him. By Granthar, what had he done? He should never have given in to her sweet pleas, no matter how tempted he was by her luscious... He shook his head. This was not the time for recrimination.

"I need to call Barig. And ask Alicia to look after the children. And..."

"Why don't you take me back to bed first?" she suggested gently, then clung to his arm again, breathing heavily. "Wait!"

He supported her as she panted through a contraction, doing his best to remain calm.

"I would say I'm pretty definitely in labor. Maybe that means this won't take long," she said optimistically when her body relaxed again, and he immediately picked her up and carried her to the bed.

Since Tyssia only had a minimal medical facility, they had decided that she would give birth at home. Barig had brought over the equipment she needed several weeks ago. As soon as Wanda was settled, he fumbled for his communicator and called her.

Wanda had several more contractions before the midwife arrived, but despite her original hopeful statement, it was not a fast labor. The afternoon wore into evening, and he could see that she was growing steadily more exhausted, even though she remained serene. He was a nervous wreck, although he did his best to conceal it.

But when their daughter finally decided to arrive, he forgot his anxiety, overcome with happiness.

His knees suddenly shaky, he sat next to Wanda on the bed and curved his arm around her as Barig handed her the baby. She was perfect, her skin as pale as her mother's and one tiny little tuft of red hair on her fragile head.

"She is so small," he breathed. His tail tentatively touched a tiny finger, and she clung to it with surprising strength. He felt that touch as surely as if she had wrapped her hand around his heart.

"She didn't feel small when she was coming out," Wanda said dryly, but she was smiling as she stroked the baby's cheek. "Isn't she beautiful?"

Barig had been wandering around cleaning up, and now she quietly approached the bed. "You should try and feed her."

"What are we going to name her?" he asked as Wanda helped the baby find her nipple.

"I thought perhaps Alice. Ouch!"

"What's wrong?" he demanded.

She gave him a rueful grin. "Nothing. I just didn't expect her to clamp down so hard. I'll get used to it."

Alice only suckled for a few minutes before her eyes drifted close. Wanda gently pulled her away, and he watched with mingled lust and tenderness as a single drop of milk lingered on a perfect rosy nipple. He captured it with a careful finger and brought it to his mouth. Delicious.

"Do you need anything else?" Barig asked quietly.

"Just the rest of my family," Wanda said, even though her eyes were heavy with exhaustion.

"Of course. But only for a quick visit, mind. You and the baby need to rest."

Barig opened the door, and Darla and Davy raced for the bed. Darla cooed over Alice, but Davy quickly lost interest and started flicking through his tool. Alicia and Rafalo were close behind the children.

"Kareena sends her love, but she didn't want to overwhelm you with visitors tonight. She said they will come by tomorrow," Alicia said, bending down to admire the baby. "She's so beautiful. What did you decide to name her?"

"Alice. I hope that's all right?"

For once, Alicia seemed to be at a loss for words. Rafalo put his arm around her as her mouth trembled.

"I... I will never forgive you for making me cry," Alicia sniffled, smiling through her tears. She bent down to kiss Wanda's cheek and pressed another kiss to the baby's soft head. "Thank you."

"Congratulations," Rafalo said, putting his hand on Mganak's shoulder.

Darla leaned against him and he wrapped his tail around her as Davy wandered back over. Wanda was a warm weight against his side, their daughter cradled in her arms, while Alicia and Rafalo flanked her on the other side. After all that time alone, he was surrounded by family, and this time, he knew he was never going to lose it.

EPILOGUE

T*wo years later...*

"I do not like it," Mganak growled as soon as the door closed behind Darla.

"It's just a group of friends going to see a show," Wanda said soothingly.

"You did not mention that it would include male 'friends.'"

"Didn't I?" She did her best to keep her expression innocent, even though she knew good and well that she hadn't. Hopefully he hadn't noticed that Tanik was amongst the group. That hope was quickly dashed.

"Nor did you mention that Tanik was going."

"What's wrong with that? I know you like him."

"I do. But I do not like the way he looks at my daughter."

"You know he would never let anything happen to her," she protested, even though she knew exactly what he meant. No one had mentioned that Tanik's people believed in fated mates, but she already suspected that Tanik had settled on Darla. She also suspected that their daughter felt the same way, but they were both far too young to do anything about it, and she trusted Tanik.

"Besides, they've got a chaperone," she added.

"By Rafalo? That old devil is more likely to get them into trouble." Despite the protest, his tone was affectionate. Rafalo had continued with his rescue efforts, but he had begun to spend more time on Tyssia, no doubt because Alicia preferred being there.

"Alicia is with them too," she reminded him. "You can't think she'd encourage any type of misbehavior."

"No, I suppose not," he agreed grumpily, still staring out the window after the group of children.

Darla had taken to her new environment with amazing ease and had no trouble making friends, although she still preferred spending much of her free time working with Mganak on his various projects.

Davy had not found it as easy, although they had eventually found a routine that worked for all of them. He spent some time with Mganak, some time with her, and some time in guided social situations. Sagat was his constant companion and had an instinctive ability to help calm the boy when he began to feel overwhelmed. Davy was never going to be exactly like the other children, but as long as he was happy, she didn't care.

Walking over to Mganak, she put her arm around him, loving the way his tail immediately encircled her waist.

"Are you going to be this bad when Alice starts going out?"

He looked horrified. "She is only a baby."

"Now. But she'll grow up, just like Darla is growing up."

"I do not want her to," he admitted. "We were going to work on that purifier tonight."

"Maybe tomorrow night." She hugged him. Mganak and

Darla had a special bond, and despite her teasing, she knew it was hard for him to think of his little girl growing up. "But right now, you're stuck with me. Whatever will we do?"

She made her eyes wide and innocent as his immediately heated in response. His tail slipped down from her waist to tease the sensitive area between her buttocks.

"What about Davy and Alice?" he asked, even as his hand dropped to her breast.

Her nipple beaded in response and she leaned into his touch. "They're both with Kareena. We have a good hour before they're home. Do you think that's enough time?"

"Barely. But I will make the best of it," he promised as he lifted her into his arms.

And his best was very good indeed.

Wanda was half asleep when she heard the front door open and Kareena call out to them.

"I will go," Mganak said. "You need your rest. You seem tired lately."

He was gone before she could respond but a slow smile curved her lips. She couldn't wait to tell him the reason for her exhaustion. Pulling her gown back over her head, she sat up against the head of the bed just as Davy ran into the room and jumped up next to her. Sagat followed him, jumping up on the other side, and she stroked his head as he purred heavily.

Davy put his head on her shoulder and snuggled against her and her heart melted. He still preferred to be the one who initiated contact but he was frequently affectionate.

"Hi, Mom," he murmured.

"Hi, sweetheart. Did you have a nice time with Kareena?"

"I played baduka with Kwaret." He frowned. "He had a new strategy."

"I am sure you will find the right countermoves," Mganak said from the doorway. Alice was curled in his arms, her eyes heavy as she sucked sleepily on her thumb. "I think this little one is ready for bed. I will start the evening meal."

She rolled her eyes. He usually insisted on preparing their meals, even though her cooking wasn't *that* bad. "I can help."

"No," Davy said firmly as he pushed free. "You should…" He frowned again, then poked her stomach. "You're getting fat."

"Your mother is perfect the way she is," Mganak said immediately, but she saw his gaze travel across her stomach, then up to her breasts. He had commented earlier about how responsive they were and she knew he was remembering that now. When he finally reached her face, she couldn't hide her smile and saw his face light up. "Mishka?"

"I was going to wait and tell the whole family together, but yes, we're having a baby!"

After she weaned Alice a year ago, they had discussed having another child but nothing had happened. Even though she was a little disappointed, they already had a wonderful family and she had put it out of her mind. She hadn't even noticed at first that she felt more tired and that her clothes seemed tighter, but the light had finally dawned. Barig had confirmed it that morning.

Mganak was still standing at the door, his face shocked. "You are sure?"

"I'm sure." She had thought he would be just as excited but he still hadn't moved. "Aren't you happy?"

"Happy?" He crossed the room in two steps, scooping her and Davy up in his other arm, his tail encircling all of them. "I never thought to be so blessed."

Davy wiggled free. "Make it a boy," he demanded as he headed for the door.

Alice cooed happily as Mganak bent over and kissed Wanda, his mouth reverent. "I love you, mishka."

"I love you too."

MUCH LATER THAT NIGHT, MGANAK HEARD THE DOOR close and slipped out of bed. Wanda had fallen asleep but he couldn't relax until their daughter was home. He found Darla wandering through the living room, a thoughtful look on her face.

"Hello, sweetheart. Did you have a good time?"

"I had a wonderful time." She smiled and hugged him, but she still seemed distracted.

"Is something wrong?"

"No. Just thinking. Where's Mom?"

"Asleep. She decided to have an early night."

The look she gave him was entirely too knowing, but thankfully, she didn't question him.

"I'll just check in on Davy and Alice before I go to bed."

"Darla, are you sure nothing is wrong? You know you can tell me anything."

"I know." She gave him a quick hug. "I just need to think some more."

"All right, sweetheart."

Her face finally resumed its usual cheerful expression. "And tomorrow night we can work on the purifier, right?"

"Of course."

"Awesome. Night, Dad. I love you."

"I love you too, Darla."

She gave him another hug and disappeared. He checked the locks and made sure the other children were sleeping peacefully, then returned to his mate, sliding quietly into bed.

"Do you feel better now?" Wanda murmured.

"I thought you were asleep."

"Not entirely." She smiled up at him, her eyes warm and loving. "Did you tell her?"

"No. I thought you would want to be the one to give her the news. You should have joined us."

"We can tell her tomorrow. Tonight I thought I'd give the two of you some time alone. You needed to see she's still your little girl."

He couldn't prevent his sigh. "Not for much longer, I am afraid."

"Maybe not. But she'll always be our daughter."

"How did I get lucky enough to have such a wise mate?"

"By salvaging what others were willing to discard." She drew him down for a kiss, and he happily obliged, his tail curving protectively over her stomach. His family was home, and all was right with the world.

AUTHORS' NOTE

Thank you for reading ***A Family for the Alien Warrior***!

We truly enjoyed writing Wanda and Mganak's story. As their sweet and steamy romance blossomed, we also explored new family dynamics, such as: teenagers, doting yet kickbutt grandparents, and a special child who was fully accepted and fiercely loved. Oh! Let's not forget our loving and ferocious 'fur uncle' because furry family members are the absolute best!

As always, we'd like to acknowledge everyone involved in the *Treasured by the Alien* series...

To our fantastic readers: We are incredibly grateful for your love and support of this series. Thank you for joining us as we tell tales (hehe) of loving, alien warriors who finally find their treasured, human mates.

To our awesome beta readers: Janet S., Nancy V., and Kitty S.: You've helped us tell wonderful stories. Thank you so much for your time and feedback. You ladies rock!

To our fabulous cover designers, Naomi Lucas and Cameron Kamenicky: Cover after cover, you both never stop amazing us. Mganak and Baby Alice have beautifully come to life because of your brilliant talent and creativity.

To our loving families: Your love and support is our bedrock. Just like our Cire warriors, we dearly treasure each and every one of you.

Again, we are so grateful that you've read our book! It would mean the world to us if you left an honest review at Amazon. Reviews help other readers find books to enjoy, which helps the authors as well!

All the best,

Honey & Bex

If you would like to be kept up to date on all the latest news—including release dates—please visit our websites!

www.honeyphillips.com

www.bexmclynn.com

OTHER TITLES

Treasured by the Alien

by Honey Phillips and Bex McLynn

Mama and the Alien Warrior

A Son for the Alien Warrior

Daughter of the Alien Warrior

A Family for the Alien Warrior

Cosmic Fairy Tales

The Ugly Dukeling by Bex McLynn

Jackie and the Giant by Honey Phillips

<u>Books by Honey Phillips</u>

The Alien Abduction Series

Anna and the Alien

Beth and the Barbarian

Cam and the Conqueror

Deb and the Demon

Ella and the Emperor

Faith and the Fighter

Greta and the Gargoyle

Hanna and the Hitman

Izzie and the Icebeast

Joan and the Juggernaut

The Alien Invasion Series

Alien Selection

Alien Conquest

Alien Prisoner

Alien Breeder

Alien Alliance

Alien Hope

Cyborgs on Mars

High Plains Cyborg

The Good, the Bad, and the Cyborg

A Fistful of Cyborg

A Few Cyborgs More

The Magnificent Cyborg

The Outlaw Cyborg

Standalone

Krampus and the Crone: A SciFi Alien Warrior Holiday Romance

Books by Bex McLynn

The Ladyships Series

Sarda

Thanemonger

Bane

Standalone

Rein: A Tidefall Novel

Printed by Amazon Italia Logistica S.r.l.
Torrazza Piemonte (TO), Italy

16751131R00112